Her knee-high black leather boots with three-inch spiked heels clicked [illegible] as she approached. [illegible] hypnotic. She reached [illegible] e velvet rope separati[illegible] ght her eyes up to sta[illegible] into his. The glance wasn't really a question. It didn't ask, *Are you going to let me in?* It said simply, *Why is this still in my way?*

Zayed lifted the rope without another thought. There was no doubt in his mind that this woman, whomever she was, *belonged* anywhere she wanted to be. Only when the rope no longer separated them did she grant him his reward. She smiled in knowing gratitude, then passed quickly into the club.

The last thing Zayed saw as she entered was a slight turn of her head as she raised her right hand to her ear, undoubtedly to rearrange her hair. He paid it no mind. Instead he focused on her perfectly toned butt as it swayed purposefully into the crowd in the direction of the bar. He turned back to the line, replacing the rope. Had he enjoyed the view for even a split second more, he would have heard her speak and probably would have second-guessed his decision to grant her immediate access, as she obviously addressed no one in particular.

"I'm in," were the two little words Zayed never heard.

Also available from

SIMON SPOTLIGHT ENTERTAINMENT

ALIAS™

TWO OF A KIND?

FAINA

COLLATERAL DAMAGE

REPLACED

THE ROAD NOT TAKEN

VIGILANCE

STRATEGIC RESERVE

ALIAS™

THE

SERIES

ONCE LOST

BY KIRSTEN BEYER

An original novel based on the
hit TV series created by J. J. Abrams

SIMON SPOTLIGHT ENTERTAINMENT
New York London Toronto Sydney

FOR KATELYN MARIE,
MY HEART'S FIRST DAUGHTER

AND ERIN KATHERINE,
WHEN YOU SEE CALIFORNIA . . .

SSE

SIMON SPOTLIGHT ENTERTAINMENT
An imprint of Simon & Schuster
1230 Avenue of the Americas, New York, New York 10020

Manufactured in the United States of America
First Edition 10 9 8 7 6 5 4 3 2 1
Library of Congress Control Number 2005933335
ISBN-13: 978-1-4169-0947-7
ISBN-10: 1-4169-0947-8

ACKNOWLEDGMENTS

My mother, Patricia, and my father, Fred, are my foundation.

Matt, Beth, Paul, Mattie, Bob, Donna, Chris, Derek, Debra, Bill, Michael, Justin, Vivian, and Ollie are my breath and blood.

Sean, Katey, Maggie, Jack, Candy, Allan, Cristiana, Carolina, Fred, Marianne, Freddie, and Tony are my family.

Sam, Heather, and Katherine are the sisters of my soul.

Chris, Vanessa, Aaron, Cappiello, Tara, Art, Jenn, Joan, Stacey, Teddy, Morgan, Abner, and Brett are my Unknown source of inspiration.

Maura is my rock.

David is my home.

Marco made this possible.

Patrick made it joyful.

J. J. Abrams and his brilliant cast and crew made it fun.

I would have been lost, once and always, without them all.

PROLOGUE

LHASA, TIBET

Faster . . .

Must . . . go . . . faster . . .

When sheer force of will combined with a strong heart and a body that had been conditioned far beyond its limits, one could do, well, just about anything. Sydney Bristow had learned this much in her thirty-four years on the planet: There was damn little she couldn't do when she set her heart and mind to it.

This moment was no exception.

Racing down the rocky, snow-covered trail,

tendrils of overhanging branches whipping at her face, Sydney pumped her arms in their punishing rhythm as the lean muscles of her thighs screamed in protest. She had chosen long ago to ignore those shouts. They were useless to her at this point. On occasions too numerous to count she pushed herself beyond the pain, the exhaustion, and the fear of physical and mental collapse. She would never know if this extraordinary mental toughness was the result of the rigorous training all CIA field agents endured, or the "Christmas" present her father had given her when she was still too young to understand its purpose. Perhaps it was a combination of the two. Where this trait came from no longer mattered.

She ran, and would continue to run, as if her life depended on it. As usual, right now it did. But the infinitesimal extra spark of strength that separated life from death in this moment did not come from Sydney's childhood, her training, or her own highly developed sense of self-preservation. It came from the fleeting glimpses she caught of the small figure running in the distance through the moonless night, the young girl she had to reach in time.

Behind her, at least a hundred meters back, she heard the *rat-tat-tat* of automatic weapons fire.

M16s. Part of her brain categorized the sound automatically. The ability to tell the make, model, and caliber of a weapon by its sound wasn't just a neat trick one pulled out at cocktail parties. As with so many of the skills she now took for granted, it came in handy at the oddest times. Like, for instance, while posing as an arms merchant when a black-market dealer decides to test your credentials by asking you to identify the handgun that is pointed at the back of your head. That had happened once to Vaughn, but Sydney had heard the whole thing through her earpiece . . . and guessed wrong. Thankfully Vaughn hadn't.

Now the ground beneath her feet seemed to tremble as another round of fire erupted behind her. The shots echoed in the distance, the sound reflected by the mountain range welling up to the north of the narrow valley that separated the snow-covered peaks from the hilltop her feet pounded.

Definitely M16s . . . at least six shooters . . . possibly eight.

Thankfully, the "trail" before her was densely crowded with trees and jutting rocks. No matter how good a shot they were, they'd have trouble hitting a moving target . . . or three.

Sydney caught a flash of pink fifty meters ahead, a pair of neon sneakers on the eleven-year-old feet of Katelyn. Sydney was 99 percent sure that one hundred meters ahead the trail bent sharply to the right, the beginning of a steep descent down the eastern ridge of the hill. She said a silent prayer that Katelyn would see it coming.

Slackening her pace only slightly, Sydney threw a quick look over her right shoulder. Forty meters back she could make out the solitary figure of her father, Jack Bristow, running behind her. As she returned her focus to the dimness ahead, another round of fire came shrieking through the darkness. This time the automatic weapons were answered by the sharp crack of the Beretta her father had pulled from the CIA safe house less than twenty minutes earlier.

Just keep them busy a few seconds more, Dad.

Katelyn had a good head start, but it had taken Sydney less than thirty seconds to close the first fifty meters that separated them. The little girl was still thirty meters ahead and only forty meters from the cliff's edge. . . .

"KATELYN!" Sydney screamed. At this point, giving away her position was not an issue.

The tree line broke less than twenty meters from the turn in the trail. Sydney got her first clear sight of Katelyn rushing toward the cliff's edge.

Faster! Every cell of Sydney's body cried out in alarm.

Ten meters to the tree line.

Katelyn continued to surge forward, her bright tennis shoes sending up tufts of new snow.

"KATELYN!" Sydney screamed again.

As if oblivious to her calls, Katelyn hurled herself forward. . . . Five meters from the cliff's edge.

Sydney reached out. She was only ten meters behind her now. She could do it. They reached the turn in the trail less than one second apart.

But in the world of Sydney Bristow one second counted.

Katelyn did not hesitate. She cleared Sydney's grasp and the edge of the trail in a breathless moment that seemed to force time to a stand still. As Sydney threw herself to the ground, breaking her forward momentum, Katelyn Magrite leaped off the edge of the cliff and disappeared into the blackness below. It seemed to take mind-numbing hours, but in reality the shriek escaped Katelyn's tiny lungs almost instantly and began to echo throughout the valley.

Part of Sydney's mind took time to wonder in how many future nightmares she would hear that scream.

Sydney's heart was pounding. She had just run almost a quarter mile full out. But as she lay in the snow, listening for . . . she wouldn't let herself even think the word "impact," the shriek continued through five endless beats of her heart. She was shaken back into real time not by the sound of a body hitting the mound of solid rock beneath, but by the hand of her father, shaking her by the shoulders as he demanded that she "Get up!"

Sydney glanced up into her father's stony face. Her cheeks were awash in sweat and tears. At some forgotten point in those five eternal heartbeats, the unimaginable pain had caught up with her senses. And even as she tried to form a coherent reply to the demand he was placing on her, the sobs began to choke her.

"Sydney, get up!" Jack demanded again, turning to face the oncoming hostiles and firing four more times into the tree line. She couldn't be sure, but she thought she heard at least two men cry out and fall. Dead tired and hamstrung by the darkness, her dad was still an amazing shot.

Sydney tried to force the pain aside. Compartmentalizing came as easily to her as breathing these days. And in her profession it was every bit as necessary to life as her autonomic nervous system. But she kept seeing pink. Not a clear image of anything . . . just the color pink.

That won't help right now, argued the part of her mind that knew better. *Let it go.*

But she couldn't.

What she could do was the next best thing. *Use it.*

Allowing her mind to focus on the bright pink, she felt a hot rush of adrenaline as the pain her mind could not contain was transmuted into rage. Pink became red.

Grasping her father's arm, Sydney rose from the ground and pulled her own 9mm from its shoulder holster, and with hell's own fury blazing in her eyes, she joined her father in spraying with gunfire the pursuers just clearing the tree line.

CHAPTER 1

LOS ANGELES (THREE DAYS EARLIER)

Sydney was still getting used to the APO bunker. Once she cleared the long dim entrance tunnel that cast its inhabitants in unflattering shades of mustard, the stark whiteness of the new CIA black ops division's headquarters came as something of a shock to the senses, even after a month. Pure white walls surrounded the white partitions that divided the space into offices, conference rooms, and cubicles. Apart from the workstation monitors displaying a variety of maps, tactical data, and research topics, the only other glimpse of color came from the bloodred leather sofa in Arvin Sloane's office.

Forty-eight hours before, Sydney had been on a return flight from Madagascar, unable to sleep. It had been an eventful few days in Madagascar—wrecking Fenton Keene's terrorist dreams and eliminating the threat of a particularly nasty new bioweapon. Whatever Keene might have been planning to do with Ice-5, however, wasn't troubling her.

Michael Vaughn was.

They'd been back in each other's lives for four weeks, back in each other's arms almost that long. Despite her repeated protestations that she wanted to take this new phase of their relationship "slow," she seemed to be falling right back into their old pattern. The job required that they spend most of their days together. More often than not they were spending their nights together as well. It was all too easy to settle in for the evening, make a quiet dinner at home, and cuddle up together on the couch. This simple ritual was as close to normal as either of their lives ever got, and Sydney had long ago decided that she needed as much "normal" in her life as she could possibly get her hands on. Michael was as kind and considerate a man and lover as she had ever known. On the surface everything was fine.

Underneath, Syd knew there was way too much they weren't talking about. A few days earlier she'd heard Vaughn confessing his sins to Meghan Keene in an effort to convince her to turn on her brother. He'd spoken about Lauren—his wife of almost two years—who only a few months ago had been revealed as a traitor, and whom Michael had killed while saving Sydney's life. He'd spoken of his anger, of his hatred, of the many times he'd imagined killing her, and then of the unsettling reality of her death.

Once Vaughn had learned the truth about Lauren, Syd had been more than a little concerned that he might lose himself in a personal quest for vengeance. True, Sydney had precious few real memories of Jack Bristow before he had learned of his own wife's—Sydney's mother's—similar betrayal. But Sydney liked to think that before Laura Bristow had been exposed as Russian spy Irina Derevko, her father had been both warmer and more emotionally available. She'd known Michael before, during, and after Lauren. She could easily imagine the demons that plagued him, and they were obviously taking their toll.

Michael was a good man. He was capable of great compassion and didn't give his heart easily. Not for the first time, she cursed Lauren for taking that heart and mangling it for her own demented ends.

What Sydney had been left with for the time being was the shell of Michael Vaughn. He still loved her. And she still loved him. If two people were ever meant to be together, theirs was surely a fated match. Their initial attraction, buried so long under the duty they had both sworn to their country, had finally taken fiery wing for a few brief months once SD-6 had been destroyed and they were both working openly for the CIA. They still had passion. But it was now tempered by pain. And for reasons Sydney could only speculate about, Michael was not yet ready to share the full force of that pain with her. That he could discuss it so openly with a stranger was difficult for Sydney. That he had yet to open up to her, his soul mate and the one true love of his life, was rapidly becoming unbearable.

For the moment, however, what would become of her and Vaughn had to be set aside. He'd left her house early in the morning with a quick kiss and a

"See you at the briefing." Given the nature of the work they both did, that would have to suffice, since the task that had brought them to the office that afternoon was sure to require every ounce of mental and physical discipline they could bring to bear.

Entering Sloane's office, Sydney realized she was almost the last to arrive. Vaughn, Dixon, and Marshall were all seated on the sofa, conferring quietly with one another. Her father, Jack, a vision of stoic tranquility, stood beside them leafing through his briefing packet.

Arvin Sloane, the antagonist in many of Sydney's nightmares, sat arranging papers on his desk as if there were nothing at all unusual about a known criminal heading up a black ops division for the CIA. The sight of him free and, most days, reasonably happy still made Syd slightly nauseated, though she was growing more accustomed to it with each day that passed, and she was certain that was not a good thing.

The only staff members missing were APO's newest recruits, Eric Weiss and her sister—*half sister*—Syd mentally corrected herself, Nadia Santos.

Syd nodded to Vaughn and Dixon as she

grabbed a briefing packet and crossed to stand by her father. Almost the moment she had assumed her place, Marshall, APO's resident technical wizard and one of Sydney's favorite people in the entire world, tugged gently on her sleeve and motioned for her to sit on the arm of the sofa beside him.

As Marshall took a quick glance at Sloane to make sure he was still occupied, a mischievous grin spread across his face. He removed a small communications earpiece from his pocket and gestured for Syd to activate it.

Equal parts amused and curious, Syd did so, but once she turned it on, she was unsure why Marshall was so pleased with himself, and unsure what she was supposed to be listening to.

"I don't think it's working," she said softly.

"Listen," Marshall replied, his bright blue eyes twinkling as his smile broadened.

Syd tried again. This time she heard it . . . ever so faintly . . . a rhythmic whoosh every few seconds.

"What is it?" she asked.

"Mitchell . . . taking a nap," Marshall replied, obviously pleased with himself.

"You bugged your baby's crib?" was Syd's next question.

"Isn't it great?" Marshall answered. "I can't tell you how many times—okay, well, twenty-six point seven times per hour—I find myself wanting to check and make sure he's breathing. Even at the office, I was driving Carrie crazy. You know: 'Hi, honey, just calling to say I love you and Mitchell and . . . uh . . . would you mind checking in on little baby Flinkman just to make sure he's breathing. I know, I know, you checked him thirty seconds ago, but the incidence of sudden infant death syndrome . . . Yeah . . . I shouldn't even think it, let alone say it, but—Oh, for Pete's sake, would you please just—'"

"I get it." Sydney cut him off with a smile. Marshall's ability to imagine and then lose himself in fabricated conversations was an endearing trait, but one that definitely required curbing. "It's a great idea," she added, handing the earpiece back to him.

"Ah, Sydney," Sloane said, "good afternoon." Everyone in the room automatically turned their attention to the slightly built bespectacled man with spiked salt-and-pepper hair (heavy on the salt) receding elegantly from his forehead. "We can begin."

"Where are agents Weiss and Santos?" Dixon asked, before Sydney had a chance. Vaughn tossed Syd a knowing wink, and Syd smiled faintly in understanding.

"Agent Weiss requested a few days of personal time to make the arrangements he will need to facilitate his transition to APO," Sloane replied simply.

"I'm sure the fact that Nadia had already planned a few days off didn't have anything to do with it," Vaughn said softly enough for only Marshall and Sydney to hear. Marshall chuckled appreciatively and Syd nodded.

Ah, Eric.

Eric was a good guy. No, Eric was a great guy. He was funny, intelligent, and had a heart the size of Montana. But he was never going to make anyone's sexiest-men-alive list, unless they were judging the total package, not just the wrapping. He and Vaughn had been friends for years. He and Syd had grown much closer in the last fifteen months. By now both knew just how many times Eric had let himself fall for a woman who was more interested in flash than substance, and who had made short work of breaking his heart. He was already showing obvious signs of falling for Nadia, and neither Vaughn nor Sydney was anxious to dissuade him. But the fact was that neither of them knew Nadia well enough yet to be certain that she would not be another disappointment for Eric. She seemed to be genuinely encouraging Eric's advances and thoroughly enjoying the new relationship, but she was also a spy. She could make anyone believe whatever she wanted them to, and both Syd and Vaughn had voiced a gentle request that he take this one slow. Unfortunately, Eric was already too far gone to listen. Nadia had him at their first hello.

Sloane cleared his throat softly, and the room grew silent. "Two weeks ago," he began, "the Regent's Clinic in Tshwane, Africa, began treating a number of local children for headaches and nausea. In sub-Saharan Africa these symptoms could indicate any number of conditions, some of them life threatening. Within the first few days a number of family members and health-care workers who were treating them were also showing symptoms. The hospital's administrators notified the World Health Organization and the Centers for

Disease Control and Prevention. Four days later these organizations were able to confirm Africa's latest outbreak of the Marburg virus.

"In and of itself this would not normally cause the worldwide intelligence community undue concern. There have been dozens of documented outbreaks of the Marburg in Africa in the past twenty years, and whenever Marburg has been found anywhere else, the cause has usually been easily traced back to Africa. The reason this has come to our attention is because there has been chatter among several black-market weapons traders in the last few months that an unknown dealer has developed a strain of Marburg for use as a biological weapon."

"When did that become possible?" Jack asked. When everyone but Sloane turned questioning eyes to him, he went on. "The natural host for Marburg has yet to be identified. Without access to the reservoir, Marburg has been an unlikely candidate for those developing new biological weapons, despite its high mortality rate."

"Apparently our anonymous designer was able to find and utilize a living strain. We believe he has been working on this since the Angola outbreak eighteen months ago. Twenty-four hours ago Echelon confirmed that the weapon's designer intentionally chose Tshwane as a target to demonstrate the strain's viability to his potential buyers."

"What's the mode of transmission?" Marshall asked.

Sloane tapped his computer and an image of a cell appeared on the monitor for all to examine. The cell's normal structures were decimated in favor of what looked like a thick black cable. Alongside the image several numbers were printed in large block letters; they indicated the virus's rate of growth and compromised tissues, as well as the blood count and other vitals of the patient to whom the cell belonged. The slide also gave a biochemical analysis of the virus and its rate of reproduction within the host.

Sloane answered Marshall's question for the rest of the room's benefit. "From what we can tell, the strain that has been developed remains dormant until introduced into a liquid medium." The moment the data had appeared on the screen, Marshall had undoubtedly seen the answer for himself.

"Marburg in a glass," Dixon said softly. "What a truly terrible idea."

"There is no known cure for Marburg," Sloane went on. "More than ninety percent of those infected die within two weeks. For a terrorist to have the ability to introduce this virus into any population's water supply is unacceptable. As of this morning we have fifty-seven verified cases. The source of this attack has been identified as a well used by a small community school."

"So where do we find the monster who did this?" Sydney asked.

"At this moment the designer's identity remains a mystery," Sloane answered, "but we have one potential lead. For the past few years Omnifam has been funding a Canadian researcher, Dr. Arthur Magrite." With the flick of a button the Marburg slide on Sloane's monitor was replaced by a black-and-white photo of a man in his early fifties. A close-cut beard and mustache gave him an air of ruggedness, but his eyes were gentle, if a little weary.

"Almost three years ago Magrite began significant research into the genetic makeup of all viral hemorrhagic fevers. Fourteen months ago he delivered a paper at a symposium Omnifam sponsored, proposing a gene therapy treatment protocol for the same viruses, including Ebola and Marburg. Very few of his fellow doctors found much potential in his approach, because gene therapy treatments for human diseases are still in their infancy. However, in the past three months Dr. Magrite has reported some significant breakthroughs. When the outbreak began in Tshwane, Omnifam immediately sent him there from his research center in Johannesburg. Within days he had reported to our board of overseers that he had successfully cured five of the victims—"

"That's huge!" Marshall interjected. "I mean, to take a treatment protocol from research to practical results in less than two years . . . And we're talking about gene therapy here, so, you know, five years would be an optimistic estimate . . . How did he . . ." Marshall trailed off as he realized that in his enthusiasm he was, not for the first time, taking the group a little off topic. "What I mean to say, Mr. Sloane, is that developing a successful gene therapy approach to curing an incurable disease should have made the local papers at the very least. I'm just wondering why we haven't heard anything about this."

"So far, no one has been able to confirm his

results," Sloane replied. "What we do know is that Dr. Magrite failed to report to work at the clinic yesterday. A subsequent investigation has revealed that his hotel and office were ransacked, and the Tshwane authorities have already declared him missing."

Sloane's interest in Magrite was suddenly crystal clear to Sydney. Without waiting for him to continue, she said, "So the anonymous designer hears about Magrite's work and has him killed to keep the price of his new weapon as high as possible."

"Exactly," Sloane replied. "If Marburg is no longer one of the deadliest viruses known to man, its viability and marketability as a weapon are adversely affected. That alone makes it reasonable to assume that our mystery man would target Magrite. What I find interesting is that Magrite is *missing*."

Sloane paused as Sydney pondered the implications.

Jack was the first to suggest what Sydney and most of the others were probably thinking. "Maybe the African authorities simply haven't found his body yet."

"I'd be inclined to agree, were it not for the

intelligence I received a few minutes ago indicating that this man . . ." Sloane paused as he changed the monitor's display again and a color surveillance photo came up. It showed an Indian male in his late thirties crossing an airport terminal. "Shahid Fardeen Aisi was spotted in Tshwane the day Magrite disappeared."

Sydney racked her brain for any firsthand knowledge of Aisi. "Wasn't he a member of the Army of the Pure?" she asked.

"He was," Sloane answered. "However, we believe he severed his ties with Pasban-e-Ahle-Hadith a few months back, when the U.S. State Department placed them on international terrorist watch lists."

"So who's he working for now?" Vaughn asked.

"Probably the highest bidder," Jack replied.

"Who appears, at the moment, to be Proto-Chem," Sloane continued. "Proto-Chem is a pharmaceutical company based in Kanpur, India, and a subsidiary of APP, a British conglomerate specializing in the development and distribution of HIV drugs in Europe and Asia."

"You're thinking that an established pharmaceutical company known for its altruistic works would be an excellent front for someone on the inside wishing to develop new biological weapons?" Sydney asked.

"It's not a huge leap," Dixon interjected, then couldn't help but add, "look at Omnifam."

Sydney felt the temperature of the room drop a few degrees as Sloane debated rising to the implied insult. A crucial step in Sloane's perceived rehabilitation, at least as far as the United States government was concerned, had been his choice to head up the world relief organization Omnifam once he had been pardoned for his work for the Alliance and SD-6. Neither Sydney nor Dixon had ever believed that Omnifam was anything other than a means to an end for Sloane. Ultimately they had been proved right. Sloane had admitted several months ago that he'd used Omnifam and the access it gave him to medical databases worldwide to discover the identity of his daughter, Nadia.

But that, like so many other atrocities, was in the past. Sloane had again managed to weasel his way back into the government's good graces. And he'd accepted his post at APO for reasons that Syd and Dixon could only speculate about, but they were certain his reasons would ultimately turn out to benefit no one but Sloane. Dixon and Sydney had agreed the day she'd started at APO and learned of Sloane's affiliation with it that the only upside, apart from once again doing field work together, was that every one of APO's senior agents had a history with Sloane and would now have the opportunity to scrutinize his every move. It was small comfort, but did ease the sting a bit.

Sloane obviously hadn't expected his new staff to welcome him back with open arms. He had asked only to be given a chance to prove himself. Dixon's public inference was hardly the first insult Sloane had endured since APO's inception, but as Sydney watched his face, she wondered how many he would accept graciously. He deserved Dixon's comment. No one could deny that. But he also needed to maintain his authority, and allowing comments like Dixon's would continue to undermine it.

For the moment, however, Sloane didn't rise to the bait. Favoring Dixon with an enigmatic half smile, he said only, "You're right, of course, Marcus. History is littered with the stories of men and women perverting noble ideas. I myself take comfort in the fact that in spite of Omnifam's association with me, and I like to think in some part *because* of it, they are now feeding more hungry children and funding more cutting-edge medical research worldwide than any similar private organization. And it appears that their affiliation with Dr. Magrite may have given us a valuable lead in the case at hand. At the moment we have nothing but Aisi and Magrite's sudden disappearance to link Proto-Chem to the designer of the Marburg strain, but it's where we are going to start."

Returning to his typically cold, detached mode, Sloane proceeded to hand out the team's assignments. "Jack, you and Sydney will go to Kanpur, track down Aisi, and determine if he is connected to Magrite's disappearance. Vaughn, Dixon, I'm sending you to Tshwane. You'll gather what you can from the clinic and get as much of Magrite's research back to Marshall as soon as possible. We need to know if the miraculous cure is real and if his work can be duplicated in the event he is dead. Marshall will review op-tech with each team en route. Your flights leave in half an hour. Go to work."

As Syndey rose from her place on the arm of the sofa to confer with Jack, Vaughn automatically followed her with his eyes. It wasn't just the grace of the motion, though he appreciated the way she moved in the same way a wine aficionado appreciated a truly great vintage. Anybody could say they liked a glass of wine—that it tasted good—and anybody with eyes could look at Sydney and see that she was off-the-charts gorgeous. But Michael's fascination with Sydney's many fine features was infinitely more subtle and refined, as it should have been, given the years of study he had put into the subject.

The casual observer would notice how the tailored white blouse and simple straight black skirt formed an elegant line from her broad, toned shoulders, cinching in ever so slightly around her slim waist to enhance the perfectly proportioned hips below it. The skirt ended two inches above her knee, but the imagination could fill in the well-defined thighs that would match her impeccably chiseled calves, which were shown to their best effect because of her classic black pumps with three-inch heels. It was a picture any Hollywood film star would have envied.

But these details barely registered with Michael. What caught his eye was the slight slope of her left shoulder as her head cocked to the right, allowing her to concentrate on Jack's quiet words while at the same time taking in every detail of the map of downtown Kanpur they were studying. Sometime over the summer she'd had her shoulder-length brown hair reshaped, and now long bangs sloped gently over her forehead, sweeping delicately back when she lifted her left hand and casually pulled the chin-length layer back behind her left ear. Her full lips were parted slightly and tinted the faintest rose. They opened a bit wider as her chin rose and she spoke softly, adding something Vaughn couldn't hear to her conversation with Jack. Her eyebrows were creeping toward one another, and the beginning of a worry line was forming just above the bridge of her nose. She was concerned or displeased with a choice they were discussing. But it was apparently a minor point. Inhaling deeply, she relented as her shoulders squared and returned to equilibrium. With that last movement, the perfection of her collarbone revealed itself enticingly, peeking out from the gap in her button-down blouse, the gap that began just above the line of her breasts and flared out at the base of her neck.

Dixon was waiting for him. They had a plane to catch. But Michael couldn't help himself. Before he left, he wanted a minute with her. Thirty seconds, if that was all they had. He was never going to be separated from her again without making sure that the last thing he told her was how much he loved her. Because the way their lives tended to go, you never knew which separation might be the last.

As Sydney folded her briefing packet under her arm and nodded briskly to Jack, she turned to leave the office. Michael caught her deep brown eyes and with a knowing smile angled his head toward the hall. She returned the smile and followed him to a quiet corner of the office.

"What's up?" she asked.

"I just wanted to make sure you were comfortable with the assignments," he replied.

"What do you mean?" she countered, her brows furrowing.

"We haven't talked much about you and your dad, and the last time you went into the field together, things were . . . well, pretty tense."

Sydney's chin dropped as she considered her reply. Finally she met his level gaze and said, "We haven't talked much about a lot of things lately."

The defensive answer was the first that rose in Michael's mind: *We haven't had time.* But before he let himself say it, he forced himself to step back and at least try to see this from her point of view. Problem was, he couldn't. He adopted as neutral a tone as possible when he replied, "What's on your mind?"

Sydney paused, her line of vision rising slightly up and to the right. Clearly this was a longer conversation than either of them could start right now. She seemed to settle for, "Don't worry about it. I just . . ."

"What?" he asked, moving closer and gently cradling her left elbow in the palm of his hand.

"When we get back, I want us to talk about you. I'm worried. Things are happening so fast . . ."

"What things?" he demanded, a sick pit taking instant form in his stomach. "You mean us?"

"No," she answered gently. "No . . . we're fine . . . we're good. I just can't help but feel like there are things you aren't sharing with me, and I don't know why."

"I share everything with you," he said simply, then added, "Everything that matters."

She favored him with a light smile and seemed to let it drop.

"I know. We're going to find our way through this. Good luck in Tshwane."

"I'll see you in a couple of days." He nodded, brushing his lips to hers and tasting her sweet, fresh breath. She drew him closer, returning the kiss more fully and tenderly. When she pulled away, her deep brown eyes pierced his as she added, "I just want to make sure you know that you can talk to me about anything."

He nodded, finally understanding. As they parted, he thought back to their return trip from Madagascar. He'd been exhausted, but as he'd drifted off to sleep, he'd heard her say, *I want you to know you can talk to me about anything.* Part of him knew then that he should have roused himself, pulled her close, and said, "I do." But the heavy wave of weariness rolling over him had pulled him under, and the next thing he'd been conscious of was the touchdown in Los Angeles. And by then her words had been forgotten, until now.

They did need to talk. Part of him knew it might do both of them good to discuss the tangled mess of feelings he was still sorting through in relation to Lauren. But the bigger part of him wanted to never mention her name again. She had taken so much from both of them. Not the least of which was time they could have spent together. To waste one more moment on the duplicitous bitch that he was sorry he'd ever laid eyes on, let alone married, seemed pointless. The past was gone; literally dead and buried. To revisit it was to bring it into his present, and all he wanted from the present was Sydney and his work. Lauren didn't deserve one more moment of his time or energy. She wasn't going to come between them again. He would do whatever he needed to make sure she didn't, whether Sydney understood his choice or not.

As the agents filed out of his office, Arvin Sloane retreated to the relative peace and quiet of his desk. He briefly considered making a personal call to Garvin Ruger, the contact who had provided the intelligence on Aisi, to confirm the content and viability of the information. But even as his hand hovered over the phone, he recalculated and determined that the call was unnecessary. Ruger was one of hundreds who owed Arvin Sloane their lives. Aisi was a minor player on the board, thoroughly expendable, and Ruger undoubtedly felt that offering Aisi up to

Sloane constituted at least partial payment on the debts he owed.

For the moment Sloane would continue to let Ruger think that. Ruger and men like him were the support pitons upon which he was currently, somewhat precariously, perched. As long as he demonstrated a consistent ability to provide meaningful and difficult-to-obtain intelligence to the CIA, his position at APO would be secure. He wouldn't allow himself the luxury of believing that just because he and Nadia had turned over their most recent Rambaldi acquisition to the United States government that his slate with Uncle Sam was anywhere near clean. He would certainly never have their complete trust. But trust wasn't nearly as valuable a commodity as power.

His gaze fell upon the framed photograph of Nadia that rested on his desk, just past the telephone. He allowed himself a moment of fatherly pride. She was beautiful, intelligent, and, like her father, extraordinarily flexible in her thinking. He had never been naïve enough to indulge in the fantasy that anyone born of his and Irina Derevko's combined genetic material would be content to live an anonymous life, far from the world of action and intrigue that he had occupied for more than thirty years. But he hadn't really allowed himself to hope that she would be so like himself either. After all, they had only known each other a few months. But they had been happy months. Things were still difficult between them, but that was to be expected. Theirs would always be a complicated relationship.

Sydney's acceptance had been a much more volatile variable in the equation, but for the moment even that seemed to be working out. Sydney was amazingly—alarmingly—adaptable. No one would have blamed her if she had maintained her distance from the child of her most bitter enemy and the mother who had betrayed her not once but many times in the past few years alone. Sloane could not imagine where Sydney had found the heart to welcome Nadia. As best he could tell, and as hard as it was to believe, that heart must have come from her father. Irina had never betrayed such sentimental tendencies in all the years Sloane had known her, but when one looked at Jack . . . well, over-emotionalism was something no one had ever accused him of either.

Perhaps Sydney had her own agenda in welcoming Nadia into her home and her life. Or perhaps, like so many times in the past, Sydney was blinded by a need for something in her life to be pure and real. Though he knew it seemed impossible, and that Sydney would never believe it, there was something pure about his love for her, and his love for Nadia. The fact that his life was and always would be dedicated to a higher purpose did not taint that love in his mind or heart. He had time. He would prove himself to Nadia, and perhaps that act would do something to rebuild his relationship with Sydney. It might be too much to hope for, but what was life without hope?

His musings were interrupted by a beep from his telephone intercom.

"What is it?" he asked, activating the speaker.

"Director Chase is on the line for you," replied the beta-shift receptionist, whose name he still had not bothered to learn.

"Tell her I'll have to return," he answered.

"Yes, sir."

Director Chase could wait. She was undoubtedly calling for an update on the situation in Tshwane, and he had plenty of good news to share. Ruger's intel alone would keep him in her good graces for another week.

For the moment he had more important and pleasant things on his mind.

CHAPTER 2

KANPUR, INDIA

Raa was busy for a Wednesday night. The nightclub on Mall Road just across from Phool Bagh Park was located near enough to most of Kanpur's major tourist attractions to guarantee decent foot traffic any day of the week. But since Bollywood favorite Amrita Patel had chosen to celebrate her twenty-second birthday in the club's VIP room a few months earlier, Raa had become the latest addition to Kanpur's exclusive "in" list. Now on any given night the line of those wishing to enter could stretch back at least thirty yards. Tonight it wound its way down the paved sidewalk almost fifty yards, and near the front the line was at least five to eight noisy-and-demanding-customers wide.

Maintaining the delicate balance between "exclusive" and "empty" was the responsibility of Zayed Dutt, and he took his role very seriously. He'd spent the past four years on the fringes of the rich and famous, serving as the gatekeeper of the velvet rope to Myst, The Club, and Fun Republic before his older brother had suggested that Raa was really the place to be if he wanted to take his career to the next level.

What Zayed wanted most was to join the ranks of the Bollywood elite as an actor. He knew he had it in him. He spent every morning developing his already sizeable biceps, and the drape of the dark maroon silk shirt he was wearing did nothing to hide the fact that his abs would have been a worthy subject for a Greek sculptor. The intimidating figure he cut was enough to ensure that very few in line would challenge his choice to grant them access or not. More important, however, he was an expert on the subject of Kanpur's social elite. He had an encyclopedic knowledge of just whose stars were on the rise and whose were falling, as well as an uncanny knack for remembering the faces of the more important directors, writers, and producers, whose pictures didn't grace the front pages of the magazines each day. But Zayed knew it was infinitely more important to be on a first name basis with this last group of people if he was ever going to stop holding that velvet rope and, instead, pass through it.

The key for anyone in his position was to make sure that at any given time the most exciting one hundred eighty-five people possible were inside. The A- and B-list figures were an easy yes. From there it got more complicated. Beautiful women were of course given a certain priority, but no one wanted to spend all night in a club where there was a disproportionate ratio of women to men. And the sad truth was, even in Kanpur, there were always more beautiful women in line than could possibly be granted access.

Zayed had an eye, however, not just for beauty. There was a more elusive, almost intangible, quality that helped him weed through the throng. The "unknown" woman who would take precedence would not only possess exquisite and perfectly proportioned physical features. There would invariably be something in her eyes . . . something that said she was confident, a risk taker. But most of all, that "something" would say that wherever the action was, she *belonged* right in the middle of it.

Zayed glanced over his right shoulder, oblivious to the advances of the six women currently at the front of the line, who had spent the last hour alternately flirting with him, pleading with him, and finally, more quietly, disparaging him. They weren't getting in tonight. Of that Zayed had no doubts. They were cute enough, and showing enough skin, but they also possessed a decidedly unattractive sense of entitlement.

The outline of the Ganesh Shankar Vidyarthi Memorial building rose above the park's central tree line, but the sight that held his initially casual glance was that of a lone woman exiting the park just across from the club. She was making a beeline for Raa's entrance, through four lanes of congested traffic.

She literally took his breath away. She could have been American or European. Her features were decidedly Anglo. But her well-tanned skin and waist-length black wavy tresses might have made that less obvious to some. She wore a deep red miniskirt, an expensive rayon blend that stopped a good four inches below her naval and barely two inches below the top of her thighs. A swath of the same fabric, but black, was wrapped around her breasts, a minimalist tube top. Floating an inch below her well-defined collarbone was a large garnet stone hung from a thin black ribbon. Around her right bicep was a red and black jeweled armband, and dangling from her ears were two matching earrings, a riot of subtle flash and color peeking out from between the curls that fell gracefully over her shoulders.

But even as Zayed took all of this in, he was drawn to her eyes. They were dark brown, and glued to his. The high cheekbones and slightly pouting lips were tinted ever so subtly, giving an air of natural beauty to the entire ensemble. Had she hesitated, even for a second, Zayed might have had time to question his gut. Had she glanced at the line or paid the slightest bit of attention to the bevy of irascible beauties near the front, who were about to be even more annoyed than they already were, he would have had time to rethink his next move.

But he didn't. Her knee-high black leather boots with three-inch spiked heels clicked imperiously on the pavement as she approached. He found the rhythm pleasantly hypnotic. She reached the entrance, glanced down at the velvet rope separating her from Zayed, and again brought her eyes up to stare tantalizingly into his. The glance wasn't really a question. It didn't ask, *Are you going to let me in?* It said simply, *Why is this still in my way?*

Zayed lifted the rope without another thought. There was no doubt in his mind that this woman, whomever she was, *belonged* anywhere she wanted to be. Only when the rope no longer separated them did she grant him his reward. She smiled in knowing gratitude, then passed quickly into the club.

The last thing Zayed saw as she entered was a slight turn of her head as she raised her right hand to her ear, undoubtedly to rearrange her hair. He paid it no mind. Instead he focused on her perfectly toned butt as it swayed purposefully into the crowd in the direction of the bar. He turned back to the line, replacing the rope. Had he enjoyed the view for even a split second more, he would have heard her speak and probably would have second-guessed his decision to grant her immediate access, as she obviously addressed no one in particular.

"I'm in," were the two little words Zayed never heard.

"Have you spotted Aisi?" Jack asked once Sydney had opened communications and confirmed her entrance into Raa.

"Not yet," she replied. "Want to give me a hand?"

"Absolutely," Jack answered.

Sydney made her way through the mass of sweaty intoxicated patrons, toward the far end of the bar that covered the entire northern wall of the club. From the corner she could stand a little above the crowded seating area and get a partially unobstructed view of the dance floor. She let her hand reach casually for her necklace. No one would have noticed as she appeared to toy with it that she was actually using her thumb to click a small switch on the back to activate a remote camera. From the comfort of the nondescript van parked on the southern border of Phool Bagh Park, Jack would now be seeing everything the wide-angle lens embedded in the garnet could catch.

One of the club's four bartenders caught her eye as she scanned the crowd.

"Looking for someone in particular?" he asked pleasantly, if a little hopefully.

Sydney smiled back. He could be helpful, but he also might tip her hand, and it was too early in the night for that.

"Not really," she replied warmly.

"What can I get you?" he asked.

"Apple martini," she replied, reaching into a small pocket in her skirt and finding enough cash to cover three drinks. She tossed the money on the bar, knowing full well she probably wouldn't still be there when her drink arrived. This wouldn't have been the first time she had ordered a drink or dinner in a place like this and ended up stiffing the waiter by rushing out without paying, usually in a rain of gunfire. But Syd tried to limit the frequency of such events. Most of the people in the food-service industry worked way too hard for their money, a lesson she had learned from her best friend, Francie—before her untimely assassination ordered by Sloane. Sydney didn't like to add to the workers' troubles by stiffing them on a tab, unless her life literally depended on it.

Returning her attention to the ever-shifting throng moving on and off the dance floor, she continued her search.

"Sydney, what's that to your right?" Her father's voice interrupted her thoughts. Turning her entire upper body to squarely face the back corner of the club, she saw a large area partitioned off with thick mosquito netting that reflected the lights alternating in shades of blue and gold in time with the music.

"VIP section," Syd suggested. "I'll take a look."

There was a bouncer at the "entrance" to the section—a gap in the fabric, where rows of stringed beads fell to the floor. Syd passed him without making eye contact. There was no need to draw his or anyone else's attention to herself unless she absolutely had to.

Following the length of the netting, she found a natural gap, just small enough for her to peer through. She was shielded from the bouncer by a mass of people returning to their table from the dance floor, but even if this hadn't been the case, Syd wouldn't have been too worried. Part of the thrill of a club like this was the opportunity it offered all of its patrons to catch a glimpse of the very important people ensconced in their more private accommodations. No one was going to stop her from taking a peek, as long as she didn't stand there staring all night.

As it happened, a peek was more than enough. Shahid Aisi was seated at the far end of a long low table filled with the remains of a lavish feast. As Sydney watched, he tipped back what was probably his fifth or sixth glass of either gin or vodka on the rocks, and drained it dry. The attentions of the two young women who were obviously sharing the evening with him did not wane. They continued to tease and flirt with him as he tossed the glass back onto the table, overturning it and spilling the ice onto the table's surface. Aisi had the bleary eyes and sagging shoulders of a man who didn't know his limits.

"I've got him," Syd said quietly to Jack.

"Confirmed," Jack replied. "I'll meet you out back in two minutes."

Taking a deep breath and plastering a practiced look of indifference on her face, Sydney squared her shoulders and approached the bouncer at the section's entrance. She could easily have taken him and five more like him down in a pinch, but again, there was no reason to make this more complicated than it had to be.

She needn't have worried. Behemoth number two, like the bouncer at the club's door, let her pass without question, and within seconds she was making her way toward Aisi through a group of young, painfully hip, and sadly desperate people.

Too easy, she thought, not for the first time that night.

TSHWANE, SOUTH AFRICA

Dixon and Vaughn had no choice but to approach the main entrance to the Regent's Clinic on foot. The narrow dirt road was lined with small wood-and-tin stalls filled with vendors hawking fruits, spices, flat breads and buns, and the occasional live animal. There was heavy foot traffic along the narrow throughway, mothers carrying one or two babies on their hips while several more children trailed behind. A few bicycles with loaded baskets wound their way through the bustling crowd. Men and women of all ages sat or sprawled along the sidewalks as if they were waiting for something—anything—better to come along.

It was hot, but that was to be expected. The dry heat was made less bearable by the constant influx of flies and mosquitoes. The locals seemed content to allow the insects to land and feed. Very few seemed to have the energy to bother swatting them away.

The clinic, which towered over the dismal landscape, was anachronistically modern. It sat adjacent to a T-intersection, rising three stories above the street level. A wide concrete staircase led to three columned archways, only one of which enclosed a pair of open wooden doors. The exterior was brick that had, probably long ago, been painted white, then left to go to seed. A small plaque set into the concrete at the entrance announced the Regent's Clinic as a gift to the people of Tshwane from Ernest and Catherine Mabuza in 1991.

Once inside, Dixon was saddened but not really surprised to note that the large waiting area was no cooler or, for that matter, cleaner than the street outside. Six rows of dark vinyl back-to-back chairs ran the length of the room, each unit holding at least the forty people they were designed to accommodate. Rickety wooden benches had been added to the perimeter. Every square millimeter of seating space was filled with women and older men, and much of the floor space directly in front of them was filled with children, who clung to their mothers' legs or napped. In the far corner a group of young boys seemed to be making a game of trapping and releasing an unfortunate rodent.

South Africa's poverty was well documented. Dixon had certainly confronted scenes of equal or greater despair in his long career. What haunted him as he picked his way carefully through the waiting masses were the eyes that from time to time met his. Some were certainly glancing at his clothes, a simple well-worn pair of jeans and a light cotton T-shirt that had been his attempt to blend in. Vaughn, the designated "patient" for their visit, had chosen a more touristy ensemble: khaki pants, a short-sleeved button-down print shirt, and clean new sneakers.

The eyes that searched Dixon's were not, as he had feared, sharp with envy or barely concealed contempt. They hardly registered his and Vaughn's obvious upper-class status and well-nourished frames. Their glances were more a temporary diversion from an otherwise endless stupor. It was something to do to break the monotony of waiting.

Once, hundreds of years ago, these people's ancestors had been proud. They had undoubtedly received pretty much the shortest end of the stick the world had to offer, but even still, their history was filled with passionate and noble men and women who had thrown off the shackles of slavery and colonialism to finally drag themselves and their people onto the world stage as a free nation.

But despite the advances of recent history, the few men and mostly women and children who filled the room seemed to have lost all but the will to keep breathing in and out. These were people who had no hope, and knowing full well that there was nothing he could do to change that, Dixon forced the gut-wrenching anger and sadness that threatened to overwhelm him into a part of his heart he would examine later. He instructed his mind to focus past the depressing and pitiful sight and on the task at hand.

"Why are there so many women here?" Vaughn asked quietly.

"The men who aren't dead or seriously ill are working," Dixon replied. "Most of the women here are probably HIV patients. They'll be dead within two years, and they know it. The best they can do is wait for rations of available medication for the children they've already passed the disease on to."

The room's only light came from four large windows on the eastern wall. Within an enclosed office at the far end, a harried nurse dealt with the people in line, and Dixon noted that the office, like the waiting area, was lit only by natural light.

"Don't they have electricity?" was Vaughn's next question.

"Even most of the hospitals considered state of the art in South Africa don't have electricity or running water," Dixon replied. "Because this clinic is private, they probably have two or three generators in the basement, but that power will be reserved for equipment and lighting in the patient's wings."

Vaughn nodded grimly. "I'll wait over here," he said, indicating the corner nearest the boys, who seemed to have lost their pet rat.

"I'll check you in," Dixon replied.

Twenty minutes later Dixon reached the front of the line. The harried nurse who wore a name badge with the word "Ntathu" written on it in permanent marker didn't even look up as she asked, "Are you here for the HIV clinic?"

"No," Dixon replied, shaking his head. "My friend and I were traveling through on our way back to Johannesburg, and he started to feel nauseated. I think he might be running a temperature." Dixon gestured to Vaughn, and the nurse acknowledged him with a nod.

"Both the clinic doctors available right now are only treating HIV patients for the next four hours. When the afternoon shift comes on, one of them will look at your friend. His name?"

"Allan Glenn," Dixon replied, and noted that Ntathu dutifully wrote the name on a much shorter list than the one she had been working on when he arrived at the window.

"How long do you think it will be?" he asked again, needing only to verify how much time he had to accomplish his mission.

"Just now," Ntathu replied.

Dixon nodded, knowing full well that "just now" was slang for any indeterminate amount of time. It could be ten minutes, ten hours, or never.

A door to the far right of Ntathu's office swung open, and a short, squat woman dressed in surgical scrubs called out the names, "Ayzize, Molefi, Rudo, Taruvinga, and Borgana."

With a glance at Ntathu to make sure she was completely occupied with her next patient, and a nod to Vaughn who was doing his best to fade into the corner, Dixon joined the line of people passing into the clinic's treatment center. He managed to make his way past the nurse and walk, unnoticed, into an adjoining hall, where he quickly located a supply closet.

Once inside, Dixon donned a pair of fresh scrubs and a surgical cap. He tied a white cloth mask around his neck as a precaution and searched in vain for surgical gloves. Whatever stock the clinic had was apparently already out for use. He shook his head sadly. He hated to move through the hospital without protection for his hands, and he had plenty of latex gloves back in the van with their standard-issue evidence kit.

I guess I'll just have to be careful.

He checked the hall to make sure he was exiting the storage closet unnoticed, then made his way down the hall, headed for a door at the end marked STAIRS in three different languages. He set a pace for himself—casual enough to appear that he was where he should be, but brisk enough to discourage unwanted questions. His first glance into a large room on his right was enough to convince him to keep walking without looking too closely. The room was filled end to end and corner to corner with at least thirty beds crammed together. A woman who looked more like a nun than a nurse casually caught his eye as he passed, but immediately returned her attention to the patient whose chart she was reviewing.

Dixon forced himself to swallow the sense of infuriating waste that rose within him, and pressed on.

Once he had reached the empty stairway, he called quietly to Vaughn through his earpiece.

"I'm in the east stairwell, proceeding to the third floor, Shotgun," he said softly as he began his ascent of the stairs.

"The office should be the fourth door on your left, Outrigger," Vaughn replied.

The office in question, the one that had been given to Dr. Magrite during his brief stay at the clinic, was midway down the corridor to his right. Had the crime scene in question been in America, the door would have been crossed with yellow crime-scene tape. As it was, immediate access was blocked by the only barrier the clinic probably had an excess supply of . . . red biohazard tape.

Dixon checked the doorknob. The door was unlocked. After a quick check to make sure his movements were unobserved, he slipped into the small office, passing under the tape and closing the door behind him.

"Ransacked" was as good a word as any for the sight that met his eyes. The only furniture in the room were a small metal desk, a wooden chair, and a small wooden table that had probably been stacked with the patient files that were now strewn haphazardly about. Almost every square foot of the floor and desk were scattered with loose papers.

As Magrite had not occupied the room for long, it seemed appropriate that there were no personal items anywhere to be found. Dixon had nursed the faint hope that Magrite had been allocated a desk-top computer that might have been tied into the clinic's network, but there was no monitor or CPU present. Clearing a path under the desk, he did find an electrical outlet that had a power cord still plugged into it.

"A laptop," he said quietly, realizing that access to Magrite's records or personal research was most likely taken with him when the office was searched. Dixon did, however, follow a second power cord to a small wireless router buried on top of the desk, and smashed to pieces. This at least offered the faint hope that whatever computer network the clinic possessed, Magrite might have stored or backed up his files through the wireless connection. It was now imperative that he find another computer on the network, or—even better—a server.

The room was illuminated by the light from a large window next to the desk. Glancing up, Dixon noted a simple lightbulb and chain attached to the ceiling, which confirmed his suspicion that the clinic's electrical supply was carefully rationed. Righting the wooden chair, Dixon positioned himself at Magrite's desk and began to search through the paperwork to see if it held anything promising.

Unfortunately, most of the pages he found contained patient histories and old lab results. There was nothing specific in the files that even referenced the gene therapy work Magrite was doing. Most likely this was the patient information that had been given to Magrite when he arrived, and which had then been transferred to his own files, probably stored on his laptop.

Dixon was about to abandon the search completely when he noted a corner of a photograph peeking out from between a few loose papers on the low table. Removing the photo, he couldn't help but smile at the face of a grinning African child, probably six or seven, in a hospital gown, waving at the camera. Seated next to the boy was a young girl, maybe a few years older, also dark skinned and smiling. The girl was dressed in a dark T-shirt, with a brightly colored scarf wrapped around her head. Turning the picture over, Dixon noted the words "Sowalzi, Day 6" scribbled on the back.

Dixon had pocketed the photo and begun to search for others like it when his attention was captured by a sound it was hard to imagine he had heard accurately. It sounded like laughter . . . a child's laughter. He rose and peered out the window, and he was surprised to see a small corner of an exterior courtyard that had been fenced in to form a playground. Faint sprigs of grass were poking defiantly through the hard dirt surface, and a small slide gave the area a more pleasant and inviting feel than the wooden benches and tables that dotted the sparse landscape outside the play area.

Five children, three boys and two girls ranging in age from four to eight, were the source of the laughter. They frolicked and gamboled about, casually observed by a woman who could only be a nurse. Dixon noted she was wearing much more up-to-date biohazard gear, including reinforced gloves. Plastic goggles and a full face mask hung around her neck, but as the nurse knelt to check a little girl who seemed to have scraped her knee after a quick trip down the slide, Dixon noted that she did not set her goggles or mask in place.

Dixon searched the faces of the children, and within moments located Sowalzi. He tapped his earpiece again.

"Shotgun, I need you to access the courtyard on the first floor. There are a number of children playing outside, and I think at least one of them was a patient of Magrite's. I'm heading back to the first floor to the restricted wing."

"Copy that, Outrigger. I'm on my way."

KANPUR, INDIA

Shahid Fardeen Aisi was having an exceptionally good night. He didn't know how many of the seventy-five thousand rupees that he'd started the evening with were still in his wallet, but there was plenty more where that came from; over two million more to be exact.

And all that for a week's work.

Now he was seated between two of the liveliest and loveliest women he'd entertained in a while. Bipasha and Preeti were both hot up-and-coming stars in India at the moment, and they were hanging on his every word as if he could give them their next job. Well, he could. But there would be very little acting (he assumed) and lots of nudity involved. It was still early, but maybe the girls were ready to head back to his suite at the Landmark, one of Kanpur's ritziest establishments, and conveniently within walking distance of Raa. *And maybe they'd ask a few of their friends to join us,* he thought greedily.

But that was the game. He'd paid a decidedly high price of admission, and he was in. No one questioned his background, his career, or his family connections. His brother, Arjun, might be content to spend the rest of his days tending goats in Lucknow, but Shahid had scraped and clawed his way out of his family's provincial existence, and now the world was literally at his fingertips.

"Another bottle of champagne, Shahid?" Preeti asked, signaling the waiter. Or maybe it was Bipasha.

"Of course," he grunted. He didn't bother to add, "Put it on my tab." It was understood that if you were seated in the club's most exclusive section, money had better not be an object.

"Shahid?" a warm and rich female voice asked from above.

"Wha . . . ?" he managed to stammer as his head drooped to the left, and past Preeti's bare shoulder he caught the somewhat fuzzy image of a pair of sleek black boots. Without risking moving his head again and the unpleasant pounding in his temples that was sure to accompany it, he let his eyes take the delicious and highly gratifying journey up the legs that were wearing those boots. Of course, they were more than adequate. Even in his state he could appreciate their firmness, their tone, and how little their owner was wearing above them.

"I don't know about you ladies," the voice said again, "but I'm not used to sharing."

Maybe it was the subtle hint of steel beneath her words, or maybe Bipasha and Preeti just knew when they were beat, but the next several seconds were uncomfortably occupied with their extrication from either side of him and their relocation to another part of the table. The next thing he was happy to be aware of: The enchanting owner of the voice had knelt to eye level on his left and was smiling in a way that promised much better things.

What had been a really good night was, it

seemed, about to get *unspeakably* good.

"Now, don't break my heart and tell me you don't remember me," the voice said softly.

Shahid tried to shake himself into awareness. It was no good. The face before him seemed to dance erratically from side to side in a way that was not physically possible. He closed his eyes, took a deep breath, and tried again, noting with relief as he gazed at her that at least her face had stopped jumping around.

It was worth the effort.

"Of course I do," he lied automatically. What did it matter if he really knew this woman? As long as she wasn't here because she thought he owed her money.

Her face grew brighter as a smile of genuine pleasure spread across it. Now he could see the American features. He took a chance.

"Bangalore?" he asked. It was among the most westernized cities in India, home of much of the country's advanced industry and newest technology, and easily the location where he would have been most likely to encounter such a creature. It was also the city where he'd spent most of his time while on Pasban-e-Ahle-Hadith's payroll.

That smile again.

"It was an amazing night for me, too," she said suggestively. "If I recall, it started with a dance."

Aisi paused. He rarely danced. Though not absolutely adverse to the exercise, he never felt he came off at his best on the dance floor. She seemed to sense his hesitation.

"A slow dance," she added.

A lascivious grin crept slowly across his face.

"Lead the way," he said, doing his best to balance his upper body on the table until he was sure he had his legs firmly under him. He needn't have worried. She put a secure and surprisingly strong arm around his waist as she led him from the private section.

Once they'd passed the barrier of beads and he'd nodded toward Dino, the amiable gentleman who for a thousand rupees had made sure he was welcome in the VIP lounge, she started directing his feet toward the rear of the club. There was no dance floor back there, just the restrooms and the fire exit.

He started to struggle, a little alarmed. An instinct honed over the many years of his profession told him this was suddenly too good to be true.

She didn't want to fight. Even as the arm encircling his waist grew inexplicably firmer, she pulled him to face her, and looked with a longing pout into his eyes.

"What's the problem?" she asked, allowing her free hand to come gently to rest on his shoulder before beginning a gentle caress of the side of his neck.

"The dance floor's that way," he replied, more alert than he had been at any other time in the past few hours.

She smiled again, almost sadly. Then he felt an unmistakable sharp prick on the side of his neck.

Her face moved quickly in and out of focus again, even as the wave of exhaustion overpowered his already dulled senses.

That was the last thing he remembered for quite a while.

CHAPTER 3

TSHWANE, SOUTH AFRICA

Dixon had returned to the clinic's first floor. He paused and reviewed his memory of the floor plan to determine the most likely way to access the playground. The clinic was arranged in a large rectangle. The now familiar south wing contained low-priority patients, or patients who were terminal and whom the clinic could offer only palliative care, because of a lack of resources. The wing to his right was much the same. At the far end, however, he noticed a door leading to the north wing of the clinic, a door that had a key-card access.

Dixon pondered this for a moment. Why would a clinic that was obviously straining under the weight of an unmanageable patient load, and that was lacking electricity to light its waiting room, need or want a high-end security door? And, perhaps more important, what was that door protecting? All Dixon knew for sure was that the play yard he had just seen could only be accessed from this secure wing of the clinic.

As Dixon was considering his options for breaching the section—a key-card duplicator was waiting for him back in the van, along with three different electronic lock-picking devices that Marshall had provided for them—a young man wearing scrubs exited through the door in question and started down the hall toward Dixon.

Keep it simple, he thought, starting toward the male nurse. When they were less than two meters from each other, Dixon abruptly crossed in front of him, as if he planned to enter a patient ward to his left, and bumped unceremoniously into the young man. Dixon had several inches and pounds on the man, and the impact sent him reeling to the floor. With profuse apologies Dixon helped the man to his feet, grasping him around the shoulders to help him up, and patting down his chest agreeably as he inquired as to the man's condition.

"It's nothing," the man insisted.

"I'm so sorry; a clumsy fool," Dixon insisted as they exchanged smiles and the man continued on his way. Dixon spared a few seconds to watch him go, to make sure he hadn't noticed that his key card had been lifted from the right breast pocked of his scrubs, along with the ID badge that had been clipped to the outside of the pocket.

As the man continued on, oblivious for the moment, Dixon hastily memorized the name, clipped the badge to his own pocket, and glanced at the key card. The fine print beneath the card's magnetic strip indicated that the card and system were the property of Omnifam.

I should have known, Dixon thought as he slid the card into the lock, received a green light clearing his entrance, and opened the door.

Despite the revelation of only moments ago, Dixon was unprepared to mentally accept the alarming difference between the north ward and the rest of the clinic. It was as if he had stepped through the looking glass and found himself at any of America's finest hospitals. Directly in front of him was a nurse's station, where women dressed in high-tech protective gear flitted back and forth between the desk and the patient rooms across from the desk and down the hall. The desk's only permanent resident sat behind a large flat-screen computer monitor. Dixon crossed behind her and saw enough of the screen to realize that she had just received, via e-mail, blood-test results that were then printed and added to one of several charts stacked at her right hand.

He made his way down the hall, noting as he did that each room of this wing was private. The beds were automated, and electronic monitors for blood pressure, heart rate, and IV controls hummed and chirped beside each patient. The only thing missing that would have been present in an American hospital was a television above each bed.

Passing a series of vacant rooms, Dixon came upon what appeared to be a surgical suite, where large lamps embedded in the ceiling would have provided more than effective lighting. Several autoclaves stood open, waiting to sterilize whatever was needed, and any number of new plastic-wrapped surgical instruments were arrayed in a series of storage bins along the far wall.

As he hurried along, Dixon noticed what appeared to be a fully stocked pharmacy, where a young woman with her back to him measured out doses of pills.

Finally his progress was halted at two large swinging wooden doors marked with RESTRICTED signs and several notices that advised anyone passing into the area to take Level-2 biohazard precautions. A large supply of protective masks, gloves, and goggles rested in a bin along the wall. Dixon grabbed a set, donned them, and entered the ward.

Unlike the outer rooms, every single bed in this wing was occupied. All of the patients seemed to be suffering from various stages of the same illness, and Dixon didn't have to check their charts to know which illness that was. Most of them shared the same characteristic rash—hard red dots, some raised, on their faces and arms. A well-protected nurse was wiping wisps of blood from beneath a young boy's fingernails. The blood indicated that his body's ability to clot had been compromised: the onset of the final stage of Marburg.

Dixon didn't want or need to spend too much time in this area. Although he was certain that these patients were receiving the best care modern medicine had to offer, and that was comforting to a degree, it was also obvious that none of these were among the patients Dr. Magrite had allegedly cured. Dixon quickly retraced his steps out of the restricted ward and continued down the hall toward the final cluster of rooms at the end of the secure wing.

The four rooms at this end were empty, but the telltale mussed sheets on the beds, and powered vital-sign monitors, indicated that they were occupied, just not at the moment. As Dixon casually entered the room to his left, he pulled that patient's chart from a bin attached to the foot of the bed, and began to read.

The seven-year-old boy's name was Landuleni, and his chart still showed Dr. Arthur Magrite as his attending physician. He had been admitted eleven days earlier and had first been seen by Dr. Magrite ten days ago. The chart contained a note indicating that the treatment protocol was contained in a file referenced only by number KM357472. But the chart did indicate that Landuleni had progressed well under the protocol. If his most recent lab work was any indication, the boy was completely cured. Dixon removed a pen from his pocket and aimed the base of it at each page as he continued reading. As he turned each page, he gently tapped the cap of the pen as if he were absentmindedly simply flicking the tip up and down. In reality this was one of Marshall's contributions to the mission, and the base was taking high-resolution photographs of each page.

Dixon moved across the hall and repeated the procedure on the chart of a female, age eight, named Thembeka, another of Dr. Magrite's successes. The third room he reached belonged to Sowalzi, the young boy in the photo Dixon had found in Magrite's office. As he opened the chart to document its contents, he was interrupted by a shuffling behind him.

"So sorry, doctor," a shy voice said, and a middle-aged matron turned to leave the room. She was draped in a dark patterned wrap and a gold flowered scarf.

"Wait," Dixon called instinctively. "You aren't interrupting. Are you a relative of Sowalzi?" he asked.

"Yes, sir." The woman nodded. "He is my nephew."

Dixon reached out to the woman, shaking her

hand warmly and drawing her away from the door in a gentle motion. He then perched himself on the edge of the bed, still pretending to examine the chart, and motioned for the woman to sit. "I am Dr. Mahluli," Dixon said, correctly remembering the name on his stolen ID tag, "and I am here to aid Dr. Magrite."

The woman's face immediately lit up. "Has Dr. Magrite returned?" she asked hopefully.

"No." Dixon shook his head and said, "But we hope to pick up where he left off. What can you tell me about Sowalzi's progress?" he asked.

"See for yourself," the woman replied. Rising, she led Dixon to the room's only window and pointed to the play yard where, sure enough, Sowalzi was perched atop the slide. As he flew down, waving his arms and laughing, no one could mistake him for anything other than a healthy and happy boy. "It is a miracle," she continued. "They say he is completely cured."

Vaughn made short work of climbing the rickety metal fence that separated the only exterior entrance to the courtyard from the alley that bordered the clinic's west wing. He noted that the south wing of the clinic had been subject to a hasty addition, probably in the last few years, and was considerably larger than was suggested by the diagrams he had reviewed prior to their arrival.

Directly in front of him, about seventy meters away, was the chain-link fence that bordered the playground Dixon had asked him to investigate.

The two nurses who were supposed to be monitoring the children were chatting with each other, giving their charges only the most casual of fleeting glances. The story the taller of the two was telling seemed to be quite entertaining, and was aided by a number of rather descriptive hand gestures that, no doubt, would have been lost on the children.

Vaughn moved closer, squatting behind one of three benches that sat empty in the courtyard. This appeared to be a rest area for the staff, though the lack of people enjoying it suggested that the clinic's personnel rarely had time for breaks. Along the wall to his left stood two vending machines circa 1960 that he presumed would expel warm sodas for the correct change. Beside the machines a cork board had been hung on the wall. Various handwritten flyers advertised for heaven only knew what.

Oddly, it reminded Vaughn of the campus where he had spent several peaceful months teaching French during what had begun as retirement from the CIA. But eventually that experience had become nothing more than a sabbatical.

He turned his attention back to the children. The nurses continued their animated conversation. If, as Dixon seemed to believe, any or all of these patients had been those Dr. Magrite had cared for, it seemed the reports of his cure were not overstated. The children were all undernourished, but no more so than any of the other hungry children he had observed in the waiting room or lining the streets of Tshwane. But these children were vibrant in a way that distinguished them from the rest of their peers.

It never ceased to amaze Vaughn that no matter how many fancy colorful electronic toys you purchased for a child, they could invariably have as much, if not more, fun with a pile of dirt. The playground's only true "toy," the plastic slide in one corner, was getting its fair share of attention, but the children not using it, bereft of anything more entertaining, sat quietly in the dirt, scooping up handfuls, building small mounds, and in the case of one little girl, apparently tasting the dirt cakes she had assembled.

Vaughn smiled as one of the nurses caught the little girl midbite and scolded her for eating the dirt. The girl was brushed off and whisked back inside, where she was probably only moments away from a harsh scrubbing.

The good news was, this left only one nurse still on duty observing the children, and she had her back to him. He cautiously inched forward, removed a small camera from his shirt pocket, and one by one captured the faces of the carefree children before him.

Dixon observed Vaughn crouching outside by the picnic benches. After nodding thoughtfully at Sowalzi's aunt, whose gaze had remained fixed on her nephew, he turned her away from the window and asked, "How sick was your nephew when he was brought to the clinic?"

"Sicker than Nobini, that is certain," the woman replied.

"Nobini?"

"My daughter. She and Sowalzi attend the same school, though she is three years older. We were certain she had not been infected. She was not at school for many days before Sowalzi and the others got sick and, of course, not for many days after."

"Do you and your daughter live in the same house with . . . ," Dixon began.

"With my brother and his wife, yes," she answered. "But Nobini started to complain of the headache, and I know she has a fever. My brother told me of the white doctor, the miracle man, we call him, who came and cured Sowalzi and the others. I bring Nobini here, but they tell me that the white doctor has gone and they do not know when he will return. It is shame. Had I brought Nobini to him one day earlier, she might yet live."

Dixon felt for the woman. It was the cruelest kind of lottery she had lost.

"Where is your daughter now?" he asked.

The woman pointed at the RESTRICTED doors, and Dixon understood immediately that she was one of the unfortunate ones he had glimpsed earlier. In all of those patients the disease was much further along, and even with this section of the clinic's better equipment there was little doubt that most of the men and women, boys and girls, behind those doors would be dead by the end of the week.

Unless we find Magrite alive, he thought bitterly. For the first time since their arrival in Africa, Dixon spared a thought for Sydney and her father. He wondered if they had located Aisi and how forthcoming they had been able to convince him to be.

But whether Magrite was alive or dead, they still needed access to his files. Although the charts he had copied were useful, it seemed that all of the specifics of Magrite's protocol were hidden in that referenced file, KM357472. Now that he was certain this area of the clinic had computers, the destruction of the wireless router upstairs made more sense. Whoever had taken Magrite had probably used the doctor's laptop and router to take all of Magrite's work. If there was nothing present on the clinic's network, there would have been no good reason to destroy the router.

Dixon returned his attention to the woman who sat, forlorn, on Sowalzi's bed, rocking gently back and forth.

"I am so sorry for your daughter," Dixon said softly.

"You will do for her what you can?" the woman asked.

"I will," he replied, nodding firmly and betraying

nothing of the fact that the "help" he intended to provide for Nobini would not come in the form that her mother probably expected.

He left the room quietly and noted that the traffic in the hall between his current position and the nurse's station had thinned somewhat. The head nurse, the one using the computer, was still glued to her keyboard and monitor. He tapped his ear again.

"Shotgun?"

"Go ahead," Vaughn replied.

"I need a small diversion."

There was a pause over their comm line.

Finally Vaughn replied, "Can you give me three minutes?"

"Can you make it two?"

"I really can't. I have to go back to the van."

"For what?" Dixon demanded.

"Trust me," Vaughn replied simply.

"Three minutes," Dixon replied, "starting now."

Sowalzi had only ever seen pictures of clowns. There were story books at his school, the school his mother and father had told him he would never be going back to. His father had learned all he needed from books at the hand of his mother, Sowalzi's grandmother. Once Sowalzi left the house of the doctors, he was going to learn, as his father had before him, from his grandmother.

But he was going to miss the picture books. Now that he was feeling better, now that his head did not feel too full to hold upright, now that he could breath without the strange sound of water coming from his chest each time he took in air, now that the itching all over his arms and back had stopped, he thought he might like going back to school and to the picture books.

He didn't know what the white doctor had done. He had a memory of his mother and father sitting by his bed. His mother was crying and his father was talking to the white doctor. So much of the last days felt like a heated dream. But he remembered the stick and remembered seeing his blood leave his arm and be pulled into the plastic tube.

That was all he remembered, until he had woken up and his mother was no longer crying.

The clowns in the picture books always had white faces. Sometimes they had big red noses and funny, floppy shoes too. He knew that the white man walking toward the fence, calling to the children, must be a clown, though, because he was bringing balloons.

Sowalzi wanted a blue balloon. But all of the balloons that the clown was bringing were white. It was no matter. A balloon was a balloon, and Sowalzi had never had one of his own.

The clown was smiling. He tossed one of the balloons into the air and then hit it gently with his hand so that it flew over the fence and into the playground. It was a strange shape, but Sowalzi didn't get a good look at it because even before it hit the ground the taller boy, Landuleni, had grabbed it and taken it for himself.

"Who else wants one?" the clown said kindly.

"Me, me, me," Sowalzi joined the others in shouting.

He heard Ms. Nomsa laugh and call to Ms. Pumla.

"You have to see this," she was saying.

The clown knelt outside the fence, meeting Sowalzi's eyes. "Have you ever seen a rooster?" the clown asked.

Sowalzi nodded. Of course he had. Who hadn't?

Then the clown took another balloon from his

pocket and blew into one end, filling it with air. The clown had not lied. As the balloon began to take shape, Sowalzi saw the round fat body of the rooster begin to form, the head, poking out from one end, and four large feathers sticking up from its back.

"And what does the rooster say?" the clown asked.

The other children joined Sowalzi in a chorus of "Cock-a-doodle-doo" as the clown again popped the rooster balloon over the fence so that it fell directly into Sowalzi's waiting hands.

"What's your name?" the clown asked.

"Sss—ssss—Sowalzi," he stammered shyly.

"What do you say to the nice man?" Ms. Nomsa asked, towering above him.

"Thank you," Sowalzi said quietly, then felt and acted on the immediate urge to run from the fence to a quiet corner where he could enjoy his balloon all by himself.

"You're welcome," the clown said. "Now, who else wants one?"

The first shout that Dixon heard from the corridor that led to the playground sounded like alarm. But the sounds that followed and surpassed it as the moments passed resolved into delighted laughter.

Dixon watched the nurse seated at the computer.

Come on, he thought. *Be interested.*

He could do what he needed to do with her there, just not as accurately. Since the only useful records he was likely to find were in the CPU that rested on the floor beneath her desk, he needed to attach the small silver node, which would transmit the hard drive's contents via satellite to Marshall, to the metal frame on the back of the CPU as close to the drive as possible. Hard to do while chatting up a nurse. Not impossible . . . just harder than it needed to be.

Finally she seemed to be able to resist her curiosity no longer. Sighing deeply and rising from her desk, she crossed to the corridor and poked her head out, calling, "What is it?"

"Come see!" another voice replied.

I guess the three minutes were worth it.

Dixon moved rapidly to the desk, reached below it, and found the back of the CPU. With a satisfying click the transmitter was set in place. Anyone who happened to check the back of the computer would only see what looked like one of many silver screws commonly found on a computer.

"Outrigger to Merlin, do you copy?" Dixon said softly.

"Loud and clear, Outrigger," Marshall replied.

"The transmitter is in place. Commence download."

"I'm way ahead of you," Marshall said.

As usual, Dixon thought, rising to leave the nurse's station. As he did so, he paused over the tree of files nearest the monitor. The labels were not patient names, as he would have expected. The first one his eyes fell on was labeled KM357474. Dixon didn't think. He simply grabbed the files and made his way toward the security door. A few moments later he was back in the main hallway, where he returned to the security closet and used his pen to capture images of every page in the files.

When his work was complete, he considered leaving the files there, but thought better of it. Returning to the hallway, he noted another pair of nurses carrying key cards headed toward the north wing.

"Pardon me," he said quickly.

They turned to him, then smiled warmly. "Yes, doctor?" one of them asked.

"Would you please return these to the nurse's station?" he asked.

"Of course," the more outgoing of the pair replied, taking the files without even looking at them.

Dixon then removed the borrowed scrubs, placed them in a nearby laundry bin, and left the clinic through the front doors, expecting to see Vaughn waiting for him. When Vaughn was nowhere to be found, Dixon headed down the alley until he found the same dilapidated metallic fence that Vaughn had climbed to enter the courtyard. He could still hear the laughs and shouts of the children in the distance.

"Outrigger to Shotgun," Dixon said, "let's go."

"Be right there," Vaughn replied.

Peering over the fence, Dixon saw the children laughing and waving at Vaughn, along with the nurses. A young boy, Sowalzi, Dixon realized, was reaching his small hand through the chain link to touch Vaughn's. Vaughn knelt and grasped it warmly for a moment, then tossed a pair of inflated latex gloves over the fence and hurried toward the courtyard exit.

Once they were en route back to the van, Dixon said, "Nice diversion."

Michael smiled and nodded, almost shyly.

LUCKNOW, INDIA

Jack parked the van on a deserted road three miles outside the small village. It had been a bumpy trek of more than an hour from Kanpur, but the combination of Aisi's blood alcohol level and the mild sedative Syd had injected into him meant that he wouldn't have been worth talking to until now.

Syd had spent the first few minutes of their journey securing Aisi to a low metal bench that ran along the back of the van on the driver's side. Heavy metal shackles surrounded his bare feet and were held in place by short lengths of heavy-duty chains that were eye-bolted to the floor. His hands were each cuffed to a similar bolt embedded in the walls of the van just above the bench. The sleeves of his black-and-red patterned silk shirt were torn at the cuffs to ensure the manacle's tightness and to annoy Aisi when he woke, if he was a man who could be annoyed by such a trivial thing. Aisi's shirt was worth at least fifty thousand rupees, or more than eight hundred American dollars, and the designer black denim pants had a rhinestone encrusted belt buckle, all of which led Jack to believe that most likely Aisi would be annoyed.

Good, Jack thought.

Interrogating someone who was already knocked off their pins was preferable to extracting information from a hardened professional who was mentally and physically prepared for what he was facing. Having been on both sides of that particular equation more times than he cared to count, Jack knew this to be true.

Sydney was now seated across from Aisi, stowing the last of her club outfit in a hard black case beneath the bench. Her long brown hair had been pulled into an efficient ponytail, and the much too revealing miniskirt and tube top had been removed, in favor of utilitarian black cargo pants and a long-sleeved black knit top. She was just checking the clip in her 9mm. Jack nodded at her in approval as she locked the safety in place and stowed the gun in the back of her waistband.

"Ready?" she asked.

"I believe so," Jack replied, moving to Aisi, whose head lolled forward, his chin resting on his chest.

"How can I help?" Syd asked.

"Make sure we have one of those canteens handy," Jack replied.

Syd's brow furrowed in an unspoken question, but she moved to the front of the van and found one of the canteens in question stowed beneath the passenger seat. Returning with it, she nodded to Jack who was busy preparing a hypodermic needle filled with a stimulant.

This was tricky business. It certainly would have been preferable if they'd had the time to wait for Aisi to "sleep off" the effects of the alcohol and drugs in his system. Adding a stimulant to the equation might overwork his cardiovascular system, as more than one speedball abuser had learned the hard way. But time was a luxury they didn't have.

Jack tapped the syringe a few times to remove any air bubbles, then jammed the needle into the hard fleshy part of Aisi's right thigh. Jack was forcing the stimulant into Aisi's system through his muscle rather than directly through his bloodstream, in order to mitigate some of the more harmful possibilities. As Jack depressed the plunger, Aisi's head jerked up and his eyes took on a wild wide expression of terror.

Moments passed and Aisi's body seemed to adjust. He began to blink rapidly and tried in vain to cry out through the heavy silver duct tape that had been strapped over his mouth. He struggled against the shackles at his wrists and feet. Finally he seemed to realize that he was in the hands of people who knew exactly what they were doing, and he fixed Jack then Syd with what was meant to be his most defiant glare.

"Are we awake?" Jack asked serenely.

Aisi roared behind the tape.

"I'll take that as a yes."

Jack moved to a briefcase that rested behind his driver's seat and removed a black-and-white photo. Bringing it up to Aisi's line of sight, he said, "The reason we are here tonight, Mr. Aisi, is to determine the whereabouts of this man. I believe you know Dr. Magrite."

Aisi didn't flinch. There was no recognition in his eyes, not even a flick of interest in the photo.

I see. We're going to be difficult.

"Here's what we know," Jack went on, as if Aisi had already confirmed his last statement. "Three days ago you were spotted at the Tshwane airport. Less than twenty-four hours later a transfer was made to one of your accounts in Kanpur in excess of two million rupees. That was less than ten hours after Dr. Magrite was last seen leaving his hotel in Tshwane."

Jack moved closer to Aisi, so that their eyes were staring directly into each other's.

"I'm going to ask you this once. If I have to ask you more than once, you are going to be considerably less comfortable than you are right now."

Jack paused to make sure his words had registered.

"Where is Dr. Magrite?"

Aisi swallowed hard.

Jack smiled.

Jack nodded to Syd, who moved over his shoulder and removed the tape that covered Aisi's mouth. Though his gaze had seemed to momentarily falter, Aisi recovered quickly, steeling himself against whatever was to come next. His tongue seemed to play over the roof of his mouth for a couple of seconds, and then Jack got his first answer.

Aisi spat what little moisture he had been able to suck from his mouth directly into Jack's face.

Jack didn't flinch. Instead he seemed to sigh, almost resignedly, and he rose from his position and again searched through the briefcase from which he had retrieved the photo.

Sydney took this pause to come into Aisi's sight line just long enough to see that he recognized her, and then she connected her right fist with searing impact to Aisi's jaw. His head slammed against the side of the van, and he let out an involuntary gasp. As she moved out of the way for Jack to return, a slow trickle of blood escaped his lips as he sneered, "Does she do all of your dirty work for you?"

Jack seemed to take the comment in stride. Seating himself comfortably before Aisi, he again locked eyes with him and said, "Look at me, Mr. Aisi. Look into my eyes." After another brief pause Jack continued, "Can you imagine a world where I would ever let anyone do my work for me?"

Aisi's stern glare seemed to deflate just a bit.

Jack raised his right hand and displayed for Aisi a small packet of what looked like a black granular substance.

Aisi's eyebrows rose involuntarily.

"I see you are familiar with your newest employer's work," Jack said matter-of-factly. Raising his head slightly to Syd, he nodded toward the canteen. She passed it to him as he opened the packet. He shook it gently, just enough to make sure that Aisi could hear the water swishing around inside, then began to empty the contents of the packet into the canteen.

"What I find ironic is that Dr. Magrite is the only man in the world who might have been able to save you from the slow and incredibly painful death you are about to experience thanks to this little packet. Of course, if you killed him . . ." Jack let the thought trail off as he started to raise the canteen lid to Aisi's lips.

Aisi turned his head away. Seconds later Syd was there, holding Aisi's head steady and forcing his lips open.

"I told you before that I would ask the question only once, Mr. Aisi," Jack said calmly. "You do remember the question, don't you?"

Aisi nodded, almost imperceptibly. Finally he stammered, "Wh-what's in it for me, if I tell you?"

"A quick death as opposed to an agonizing one where you will literally bleed out from every orifice in your body before your lungs fill with fluid and you drown," Jack replied. "If I am very, very pleased with your answers."

The canteen was millimeters from Aisi's lips when he shouted, "Wait!"

Jack smiled for the second time since Aisi had woken.

CHAPTER 4

LOS ANGELES

Marshall sat before his computer monitor, unable to believe what he was seeing. He had spent the past four hours digesting the files Dixon had sent from Tshwane. He had double-checked his analysis with Dr. Hopi, one of the CIA's top medical researchers. He now knew two things that he hadn't known four hours ago, and both of them seemed equally implausible.

First, Dr. Arthur Magrite had, in fact, designed a gene therapy protocol that was capable of eradicating the Marburg virus.

Second—and this was the one Marshall was really having difficulty swallowing—Dr. Magrite was smarter than he was. He had to be.

Marshall shook his head for the hundredth time.

"How?" he said aloud, also for the hundredth time since he had started working on the Magrite files.

The computer download had contained some interesting information. The hourly lab results of each of the five patients that Magrite had successfully cured were charted in mind-numbing detail. In each case a marked reduction of the virus's ability to reproduce had been noted between ten and twenty hours after the new genetic code had been introduced into the patient. Relief of symptoms followed within twenty-four more hours. In five out of five patients seventy-two hours after the introduction of the appropriate genetic material, the body's immune system had effectively wiped out the invading Marburg virus, and the patients were restored to better health than they'd had before the initial infection, due to their strengthened immune systems.

This in and of itself was extraordinary. This was

gene therapy exactly as it had been imagined on paper. What made it difficult to accept was that with the exception of a few isolated cases, gene therapy trials that had begun as early as 1990 had all shown significantly more complex and less promising results. Marshall didn't have to have the genius level IQ that he did to understand the broad strokes of why.

The human genome had yet to be completely mapped. True, researchers had more than 90 percent of it, but that still left an awful lot of genetic material that was still on the drawing board. More important, the genes that were mapped were not yet completely understood in all of their interactions. History had shown thus far that it wasn't as simple as gene 1 is malfunctioning, so let's replace gene 1 with a perfect copy and solve the problem. Gene 1 might be malfunctioning, but genes 14 and 31 might have mutations that were specific to that person that would be affected by any change to gene 1. So putting a perfect copy of gene 1 into a sick patient could solve the problem. Or it could create bigger problems on genes 14 and 31.

Marshall understood, probably better than the good Dr. Hopi, what would eventually have to happen for gene therapy to be the magical cure-all it was promised to be. A complete map or blueprint of the genetically perfect human being, that was, a human whose genes were all functioning optimally, would have to exist. Of course, no human being on the planet was going to have the perfect genome. It would have to be extrapolated from many people, none of whom shared the same genetic defects. But that was only the first part of the problem.

The next step would involve the patient, the individual suffering from a disease that could theoretically be cured by genetic alterations. Eventually any individual suffering from a disease would have to have their entire specific genome mapped. Billions upon billions of base pair sequences would be fed into a supercomputer and cross-referenced against that theoretical perfect genome. Once the gene that was malfunctioning was identified, the rest of the genome would have to be analyzed so that interactions between the target gene and other possible mutations could be identified and accounted for before any new genetic material was introduced.

Further, the delivery system, or "vector," for the new genetic material would have to be analyzed against the specific person's genome to ensure that the body would not reject it or destroy it. Since viruses were the most common vector being tested at the moment, and a normally functioning human immune system was designed to eradicate any viruses it found before they had a chance to reproduce, designer vectors were the optimum solution.

But as Marshall well knew, even if he were the one working to develop such a vector, it would take months to create, even with the theoretical perfect genome and the most powerful computers at his disposal. Then it would have to be recreated for each new patient.

That Magrite had cured one person in two weeks was a miracle. That he had cured five seemed impossible.

But the evidence in front of him showed in no uncertain terms that Dr. Magrite had cured these patients, and for the life of him Marshall didn't understand how.

He was certain that the answer to that question was partially contained in the numbered files that Dixon had copied, which he'd transmitted shortly after he and Vaughn had left the clinic. Each file contained several segments of the patient's genome and the genes that were targeted for therapy. Each file also contained a blueprint of the vector designed for that patient. The problem was that each vector was different. Each one seemed to take into account potential mutations on other genes that would adversely affect the patient's recovery. Magrite had, in effect, created the elusive designer vector and implemented it successfully.

Marshall had noted that Dixon's report indicated Magrite had probably kept most of his research on a laptop that was missing from his office. It had taken Marshall only a few seconds to analyze the clinic's network and recognize the IPN for that laptop. The laptop in question had also been analyzed, at least in its processing power, and the hard cold reality was that there was no way Magrite had mapped one complete genome, let alone five, on the relatively lightweight computer he could have purchased in any retail store.

Magrite had another machine somewhere doing his calculations, math that no computer yet invented would be able to accomplish in the time it had taken Magrite to cure his patients.

"How?" Marshall asked himself again.

He hated that question. Not just because any

minute now he was scheduled to go online with Dixon, Vaughn, and Sloane and update them as to his findings. He hated it because he had never, in all his years with the CIA, come across a question that seemed to have no answer. Sometimes the answer was hours or days or even, in particularly brutal cases, weeks away, but it was always there.

This answer wasn't.

There was a piece of this puzzle they were all missing, and Marshall had no idea where they were going to look to find it.

God, don't let Magrite be dead, Marshall thought. This was one of those questions that was going to keep him awake at night. Between this and making sure little Mitchell kept breathing, Marshall might not sleep again for a very, very long time.

TSHWANE, SOUTH AFRICA

"Just . . . just start at the beginning, again," Vaughn said calmly. He and Dixon had spent the past half hour discussing Magrite's files with Marshall via a video conference bouncing off the CIA's secure satellite network, and Vaughn still didn't have answered to his satisfaction the two most basic questions that he and Dixon had posed.

The hotel they had designated as their base camp for the evening was luxurious by Tshwane's standards, which was to say it had running water and electricity. Vaughn was seated on a hard wooden chair before a bad reproduction of an eighteenth-century French writing table, where their communications equipment had been set up. Dixon had vacated the deep cushioned love seat in favor of pacing to and fro behind Vaughn. Once they had returned from the clinic, they had shared a quick snack in the hotel bar and managed to get a few restless hours of sleep while they waited on Marshall. Marshall had agreed to contact them when he had a definitive answer as to whether or not Magrite had succeeded, and if so, how.

It wasn't that Vaughn was overly anxious to head back to Los Angeles. He was, of course. But he wasn't so anxious that he would abandon his part of this mission. He wouldn't leave until he was absolutely certain that he and Dixon had done all they could to figure out if anything in Dr. Magrite's files contained a potential clue as to the doctor's current whereabouts or abductor. Sydney had been assigned the much more potentially dangerous part of the mission. Confronting a known terrorist and forcing him to provide intelligence about another terrorist was never a walk in the park. Even though Syd was partnered with Jack, and Vaughn knew full well that Jack would willingly die before he let anything happen to his daughter, part of Vaughn's frustration in this moment undoubtedly arose from the fact that if anyone was going to be out there watching over Sydney, he wanted to be that person. All he could do right now to make Sydney's life easier and potentially safer was to complete as thorough an analysis of Magrite's work as his limited understanding of biochemistry and genetics would allow. Unfortunately for both him and Dixon, Marshall was obviously so wired by what he had found—and its implications—that he was having difficulty explaining himself in anything other than the most technical terms.

Though Vaughn never liked to admit it, he always appreciated Weiss's presence in the briefings, particularly those that included Marshall, because Eric never hesitated to call Marshall on his tendency to speak science instead of English. Vaughn had never admitted to anyone that Eric usually managed to do this at the exact moment

Vaughn's brain was also starting to hum with an inability to process what he was hearing. Nor had he admitted that he would never, no matter how overwhelming the hum had become, willingly have been the first in the room to acknowledge publicly that he didn't understand what Marshall was saying. Sydney, Jack, and, for that matter, Sloane never seemed to have difficulty keeping up. Vaughn would be damned if he would ever flaunt any inadequacy in this group, though in no other aspect of his life did he ever feel intellectually threatened.

Where the hell is Weiss when I need him? Vaughn thought, as he began to massage the base of his neck and focus his concentration again on Marshall's face, which appeared to be every bit as frustrated as his. He knew Dixon was feeling the pressure too, but was relieved when he stopped pacing and brought his face into the camera's range so that Marshall would be looking at both of them from his optical receiver back in Los Angeles. He spoke next, again straining to remain patient.

"Did Magrite cure Marburg, or didn't he?" Dixon asked.

Marshall paused, as if doing his best to present

the most clear and concise response at his disposal.

"Yes," he said, nodding.

Vaughn and Dixon emitted a simultaneous short sigh.

Excellent. Question number one: answered.

"And no," Marshall added.

Dixon put a little too much force into the punch he gave the back of Vaughn's chair before he resumed his trek around the room.

"It can't be both, Marshall!" he said forcefully.

"Yes it can," Marshall replied defensively.

"How?" Vaughn demanded.

Marshall paused again.

"Okay . . . think of it like this—," he began.

"No, no more metaphors," Vaughn interrupted.

"But if you don't understand the technical terms, and you don't let me use examples—"

"Wait a minute," Vaughn interrupted again. He suddenly realized that part of their problem for the last half hour was not Marshall's answers but the questions they were posing.

"Let me ask you this much," he continued.

"What?" Marshall said.

"Did Magrite cure the five patients that he reported were cured?" Vaughn asked.

"Yes," Marshall replied unequivocally.

"But that doesn't mean he's cured the virus?" Dixon asked impatiently, coming to a stop again behind Vaughn's chair.

"No," Marshall replied just as emphatically.

Here's where it gets tricky, Vaughn thought.

"Now, as simply as you can, explain why," Vaughn said calmly.

Marshall was obviously struggling to distill the information rushing through his head into the most basic answer he could muster.

"Because the cure is specific to each patient."

"Okay," Vaughn said. "How?"

"The problem is that Marburg isn't a genetic disorder," Marshall began. "It's not like cerebral palsy or any of a couple hundred other known genetic abnormalities that result in a disease process. No matter what your genetic code looks like, if you are exposed to Marburg, you are going to get sick."

"Okay." Vaughn nodded. *So far so good.*

"From a gene therapist's point of view it's more like some kinds of cancer," Marshall continued.

"In what way?" Dixon asked over Vaughn's shoulder.

"In that certain genetic expressions can make a person predisposed to certain kinds of cancer if they are exposed to other environmental factors. Or some people are simply more likely to get certain cancers if they have a family history of the disease, because they probably share a genetic predisposition that we haven't yet identified or don't know how to screen for yet."

"So some people are more likely than others to get Marburg?" Dixon asked uncertainly. "You just said that everyone exposed to the virus would get sick."

"Right, but not everyone exposed to the virus, *dies* from it," Marshall said.

Ahhh. Vaughn had it. *Light at the end of the tunnel.*

"So Magrite created a gene therapy protocol that heightened the patient's immune system?" Vaughn asked, knowing full well he was probably getting way ahead of himself but anxious nonetheless to get to question two: How did Magrite do what he did?

"That would have been the next logical step," Marshall agreed, and Vaughn threw a glance at Dixon that plainly read: *Hah! I got one.*

Dixon rolled his eyes as Marshall continued.

"My guess is that he looked at the genetic makeup of anyone he could find who had ever been exposed to a viral hemorrhagic fever and survived. We know that there are no drugs that can treat the virus, or even really relieve the symptoms, so that wouldn't have been a factor. He would have to have found a genetic combination that predisposed the individuals he was looking at to survive a Marburg infection."

"And then he would compare that to the code of the sick individuals and, using the difference, come up with the gene therapy?" Dixon asked.

"Sure," Marshall said, and nodded. "Except that with today's technology and the amount of time he had, there's no way Magrite did that for five people in less than two weeks. Honestly, there's no way he did that for five people in less than two years. I mean, maybe if he had one of those time twisty thingies—What the hell was that called? Oh yeah, a time *turner*—and then he could, you know, just keep going back and reliving the same day over and over again until he had it, and then it wouldn't matter how many years he spent. You know, come to think of it, a wormhole in the fabric of—"

"The point, Marshall," Vaughn said, nudging him back on track, "is that, impossible as it may seem, Magrite did develop a cure for each individual patient he treated, but the cure would only work for those patients. Each person who was brought to him with the disease would have to start at the beginning, with the genetic analysis, before a treatment could be developed for them."

"That's right," Marshall said. "So . . . you tell me . . . is that a cure or not?"

"Yes and no," Vaughn and Dixon said in unison.

"Which is what I said in the first place," Marshall couldn't help but add.

"Okay," Vaughn continued, thrilled that they had finally gotten this far, "so he's developed a custom cure for each patient based on their genetic profile. How did he do it?"

"I don't know!" Marshall shouted. "Why do you think I—"

"It's okay, Marshall. We'll figure it out," Vaughn said as soothingly as possible. "Where would he have started?"

"Blood sample."

"Okay, he looks at the blood cells and develops

a complete genetic blueprint from that," Vaughn said encouragingly.

"Right, that's not so hard."

"And you found part of the patients' genetic codes in the files I sent?" Dixon asked for confirmation.

"Right, the relevant sections," Marshall replied, "which were different for each patient."

"So he would have used a computer to analyze the genetic code and design the specific cure?" Vaughn asked.

"Right," Marshall answered, "which is where we run into problems."

"How is that so unusual?" Vaughn asked. "When I was infected with the blood disease that Irina Derevko developed—"

But Marshall was way ahead of him. "That was different. That was a synthetic virus. To program a computer to provide a genetically specific cure for something you created is very different from creating a cure for something you don't have the host for."

Vaughn thought back to the briefing that had taken place less than twenty hours earlier . . . to Jack's comments about Marburg's reservoir.

"Maybe Magrite isolated the reservoir," he suggested tentatively.

"No way," Marshall replied. "If he had a sample from the host, he would have worked on an antivirus or a vaccine, right after he accepted his Nobel Prize. He didn't have the reservoir."

"Then he wrote a program that would allow his computer to analyze the genetic code of the patients and determine the best potential therapy to heighten each patient's immune response," Vaughn concluded.

"For which he also won a Nobel Prize that none of us heard about?" Marshall asked. "Right after he announced that he's also found the cure for AIDS, the common cold—"

"I get it," Vaughn said. "But that doesn't change the fact that he did it, somehow. He was able to look at the genetic code of his patients and see the change that would have been most effective for them."

"Combination of changes," Marshall corrected him. "That's what makes it so unlikely we are looking at a computer-generated cure. If we knew what the perfect human genome was supposed to look like and absolutely understood the job and interaction of every single gene in the human body, a computer could do what you are suggesting. But we don't. It's like the guy could look at billions of pieces of a puzzle and see, intuitively, which pieces went where without even knowing what the finished picture should look like. But no matter what, each time, the picture turned out perfect."

Vaughn now understood why Marshall was so frustrated. There was no answer to question number two, at least no answer that made any sense.

"Then we're missing something," Dixon interjected. "What could it be?"

"Maybe he could do math in his head that Einstein couldn't," Marshall said, then trailed off, turning his head slightly and staring off into empty space as he seemed to consider something intriguing and previously unexplored.

"Marshall?" Vaughn said.

No reply.

"Marshall, what is it?" Dixon asked more forcefully.

Marshall shook his head and returned his gaze to the camera at his end of the conference.

"Nothing," he replied. "I mean, it's *so* not likely."

"What?" Vaughn asked, truly intrigued.

But before he could coax an answer out of Marshall, their screen split and Sloane's face appeared on the entire right half of it. Marshall remained quiet on the left, his eyes widening as he took in Sloane's appearance.

"Gentlemen," Sloane greeted them. "I've just received word from Jack and Syd that they were able to obtain the information we required from Mr. Aisi. He was never introduced to, nor did he ever speak to, the individual who hired him, but Aisi did confirm that he was hired not to kill Magrite, only to kidnap him and bring him to a drop point in Kanpur. They are following up that trail now and will hopefully have Dr. Magrite back in our hands within the next few hours—"

"That's great," Marshall interrupted enthusiastically.

"I take it you've had some success of your own?" Sloane asked.

"Yes, sir," Vaughn said flatly.

"Marshall briefed me on the broad strokes. It's intriguing, isn't it?" Sloane asked. "I guess we won't have answers to all of our questions until we're able to talk directly to Dr. Magrite, will we?" he continued.

"So we'll be returning to Los Angeles right away?" Dixon asked.

"Not quite," Sloane replied. "We have another lead, and in the interest of exhausting all of our possibilities, I'm sending you both to Soweto."

"Why there?" Dixon asked.

"An in-depth analysis of Magrite's financial records showed regular monthly transfers to an account in Johannesburg. The transfers were rerouted to a private individual in Soweto every month for the past eleven years. The account belonged to a British expat named Cecilia Minden."

"Girlfriend?" Vaughn wondered aloud.

"Doubtful," replied Sloane. "She's seventy-nine. But then there's no accounting for taste. Much more interesting than Magrite's sexual proclivities, however, is the fact that Minden's deceased husband, Theodore, served briefly on APP's board of directors, and was apparently a long-time friend of Magrite's until his death thirteen years ago. The fact that APP can be financially linked to Magrite's kidnapper might give us a clue as to how the biological weapon's designer was able to get to Magrite so quickly after his work started to show promising results."

"Were the circumstances of Theodore Minden's death unusual?" Vaughn asked.

"Heart disease," Sloane replied. "The autopsy didn't reveal anything out of the ordinary. But Minden was considerably better off than Magrite, which raises the question, Why would Magrite feel it necessary to continue to provide in some way for Minden's widow?"

After a brief pause during which they all considered this, Sloane brought the conference to a close, "Wheels up in forty minutes, gentlemen. Report in as soon as you've found Cecilia Minden."

With a slight nod Vaughn signed off on the call and turned to Dixon, who was already collecting his gear.

"So what's Soweto like this time of year?" he asked.

"How the hell would I know?" Dixon replied. "My guess would be hot."

KANPUR, INDIA

Once he had given them what little real intel he could offer, Aisi had been left to the tender ministrations of one of APO's transport teams. Sydney had found it difficult to tell if he'd been more angry or relieved when Jack had failed to kill him quickly, as promised. The anger she could almost understand. Men like Aisi needed to feel that they controlled as much of their world as possible. So did women like Sydney, for that matter. Aisi had believed her father. She was certain of that much. He had given them the details of his contract on Magrite so that he could determine the mechanism of his death. True, slow and horrible or quick and painless wasn't much of a choice, but when that was all that was on the table . . .

Sydney rested a bit easier knowing that for now at least one more hostile was in custody. Two more would spring up tomorrow to take Aisi's place; that was the frustrating math of modern day terrorism, but that would be a battle for another day.

"Are you ready?" Jack asked from the driver's seat of the van.

Sydney pulled a dark green tank over her knit top in an effort to tone down her recon attire so that she could blend more easily into the academic population she was about to infiltrate. She took a moment to double-check the contents of her black leather backpack and replied, "Yep."

"I still think we should both go in on the retrieval," Jack said.

Sydney gave her father a slight smile. He knew the gory details of every op that Sydney had ever filed a report on, and many that she hadn't. He'd seen Sydney take down multiple hostiles all by herself on more missions than either of them cared to count. Once they knew exactly where Magrite was being held and what his security team looked like, Sydney might change her mind, but for now she firmly believed that Jack's desire to accompany her onto the campus of Kanpur University was driven by a sense of parental protectiveness more than the requirements of the mission at hand.

"I'll be right back," Syd said, then jumped out of the van.

Her suspicions were confirmed when Jack raised no further protests and simply moved to assume his position in the van's rear, where he would monitor Syd's every move from the mobile operations center they had set up once Aisi had been taken off their hands.

It was midafternoon on the busy campus, and as Syd joined a group of students queued up before the guard kiosk at the university's western entrance, she pulled her student ID from her backpack and assumed a stance that mimicked the rest of those waiting in line, bored and very put-upon by all of this unnecessary security.

As she waited, she reflected on the fact that she and her father had said nothing to each other in the past twenty hours that hadn't been required for the mission. There were times in Sydney's life when this would have been unusual. She had grown closer to her father than would have been possible before she had become a double agent within SD-6 and learned that her father was also a double agent for the CIA, working to bring down the Alliance. Unfortunately, they'd recently hit one of their more daunting rough patches.

Sydney had learned several months earlier that Jack had obtained clearance to have her mother, Irina Derevko, assassinated. Sydney's feelings for her mother had been complicated, but she had been unprepared for the horror and despair she'd felt when she found out about her mother's death, particularly on her father's orders. It wasn't that she trusted her mother, or believed that her mother loved her unconditionally. It was largely that there were still a million questions she had fully intended to ask Irina one of these days, and now she was never going to have that chance.

More surprising, in some ways, was the fact that when Sydney had completely frozen her father out of her life following this revelation, Jack had accepted this. Rather than add to Sydney's pain, he didn't tell her that he had ordered Irina's assassination only because he had received intelligence that Irina had put a contract on Sydney's life, a contract that was only invalidated when Irina died.

Sydney had learned the whole awful truth only a few weeks earlier, and since then, her anger with Jack had resolved itself into an uneasy knot in her stomach, equal parts understanding and pain. They'd been too busy since then to really discuss the issue in depth, and now Sydney was unsure whether or not she even wanted to.

She appreciated the fact that Jack seemed to be leaving the next move up to her. She couldn't be angry at him for trying to protect her. She could understand the lengths to which he had gone, and truly believed that he had not chosen his course to satisfy any need he might have had for personal revenge against Irina. The past few years seemed to have brought Sydney's parents closer than they had ever been. For the first time, they had been able to face and interact with each other as themselves, not their work-required aliases. Despite the many sins they might never be able to forgive, Irina and Jack had seemed to meet upon the common ground of their love for Sydney.

This made everything Irina had done since she'd escaped CIA custody, including ordering Sydney's assassination, all the more impenetrable and painful. But as with so many pieces of Sydney's life, the truth behind her mother's actions seemed destined to be a mystery she would never fully solve.

No, she no longer blamed her father for what he had done. But she still couldn't seem to think about reconnecting with him without also delving into that dark place in her heart where he and Irina and Sydney were irrevocably bound together. She had neither the time nor the energy for it now. Maybe Jack didn't either.

It was funny, in a way. She had started the previous day nursing her pain about Michael's choice to keep his feelings from her. At the same time, she was withholding the possibility for release and closure from her father. Not because she was angry or confused; she was simply too exhausted to go there right now. In a flash of unwelcome insight it dawned on her that perhaps what Michael was going through was no more complicated than this.

Once through the security gate, Syd refocused her attention on the task at hand and walked briskly across the small parklike common area bordered by student dormitories on both sides, and emerged at a crosswalk. On the other side of the narrow two-lane road were the backs of several academic buildings, including the university's main library. Sydney considered the three-story gray cinder-block building and opted to gain access to the roof she needed by the least dramatic means possible.

Making her way along a well-landscaped path that ran between the library and the music building, which stood on her right, Sydney soon found herself stepping into the heavy foot traffic that wound its way across the main mall.

Less than three minutes after entering the library, two security cameras and a fire alarm attached to the roof access door in the northwest stairwell had been disabled, and Sydney was perched on the roof behind a long silver duct that adequately concealed her position. As she pulled her infrared binoculars from her pack, she was accompanied by the pleasant strains of what sounded like a Haydn sonata for piano, coming from one of the practice rooms in the building next door.

Smiling slightly, Sydney raised her binoculars and trained them on the Proto-Chem Research Center located directly across the mall from the library. The medical laboratory had been a gift from the pharmaceutical giant six years earlier. The four lowest floors were devoted to small classrooms and labs for the lucky researchers who had been granted fellowships. The three upper floors, however, were currently designated for private research projects and, from the looks of things, weren't all that useful to either Proto-Chem or the university at the moment. Though the lower floors were filled with the kind of heat signatures and movement you would expect—small clusters of students seated together a few meters from an individual standing to lecture, two to four people working in each of the more obvious labs—the fifth and seventh floors were completely lifeless. That seemed unusual for midday during the academic term, until Syd caught a clear image of activity near the southeast corner of the sixth floor that made the other vacancies understandable.

"Phoenix to Raptor," Syd said softly, activating her earpiece.

"Go ahead, Phoenix," Jack replied.

"I'm looking at the sixth floor of the research center. The floor is deserted, but in the southeast corner there's a laboratory space with one individual working, seated, and outside there are three more heat signatures, pacing and clearly armed."

"Just three guards?" Jack asked.

"I know," Syd replied. "It's a lot of trouble to go to if you're not going to protect your asset any better than that, but then again, they probably aren't expecting too many people to miss Magrite."

"You want backup?" Jack asked in a way that suggested he already knew the answer.

"Just keep the motor running," Syd replied. "This won't take long."

CHAPTER 5

Sydney considered her options as she crossed the mall that separated the library from the research center. She could easily just try the "lost student" gambit, approaching the guards with just enough naïve helplessness to lull them into complacency before she dropped them to the floor and retrieved Magrite. Had rescuing the doctor been the only priority in play, that probably would have been her first choice.

But something about the entire scene was suggesting more caution. At the end of this day APO needed a name and a face for their mysterious weapon designer, and if Magrite had been kept as much in the dark as Aisi, which seemed possible, a straight extraction wasn't going to get them where they needed to be.

As Syd settled on her Plan B, she took comfort from the fact that Magrite had been kept alive this long. Their ultimate target obviously needed Magrite for something. Sydney hoped that Magrite wasn't being used to strengthen the weapon strain in order to counter whatever cure he had developed, but she couldn't imagine too many alternate scenarios that justified kidnapping Magrite rather than executing him.

Entering the research center's main lobby, Syd took an immediate left and headed for the building's northwest staircase. Though the stairs were external to the building, the only access points were off the lobby of each floor. As she began her ascent to the seventh floor, she was joined on the stairs by several students moving quickly between classes.

For the briefest of moments Sydney was a graduate student again. She remembered fondly that brief bright period in her life when she honestly believed she was pursuing her degree in order to leave the world of covert operations behind her and assume a real and normal life. Her days as a student had been more challenging than most. Managing the workload between missions had driven her to distraction, but the understanding and encouragement of a few teachers, along with her father's surprising admission that he believed Sydney could become one of those teachers that students would always remember, had infused her waning spirits at just the right times. That was what had enabled her to see the work through to graduation. Though she had since realized that she was probably not going to put the CIA behind her for many years, she was still glad she had earned her master's, and the right to pursue a career as a teacher someday . . . perhaps.

Pausing to pretend to pull something from her backpack, Syd waited until the staircase was deserted before she completed the climb to the seventh floor. She was certain that none of her fellow students would be heading to that floor, but didn't want to attract undue attention. Once she reached the door, she was not at all surprised to find that it was locked. Retrieving a standard lock-picking kit from the utility case Marshall had inserted into the heel of her boot (it also contained a small pin-light, a backup earpiece, a dime-size switch-operated incendiary device for diversionary purposes, and tiny wire clippers), Sydney quickly rolled the tumblers into place and slipped inside the door. As she stowed the lock picks, she thought briefly that the entire Swiss army had nothing on APO's Marshall Flinkman.

The utilitarian hallway before her was dimly lit and, as she had expected, empty. She moved quietly to a nearby lab and entered, scanning the ceiling for ventilation. A four-by-two vent cover in the far corner was exactly what she was seeking, and Syd quickly climbed on top of a sturdy worktable and removed the vent cover.

As she was unwilling to risk alerting the guards to her presence by accessing the sixth floor directly, Syd had her choice of using the building's ventilation ducts to either climb up from the fifth floor or climb down from the seventh. She had opted for down because it was easier to attach a rope to an existing ceiling support beam and move down than shoot blindly for such a beam and climb up.

Once she reached the crawl space just above the sixth floor, she cut a hole in the duct wide enough to pull herself out, and patched the duct as quickly as she could. She didn't know how bright Magrite's guards were, but had she been in their place, a sudden shift in the air conditioning that was not explained by a look at the building's thermostat would have activated her internal alarms.

Once clear of the ventilation duct, Sydney played her flashlight over the crawl space. There were support beams just wide enough for her to maneuver from her present location to the far southeast corner above the lab where she believed Magrite was being held. For good measure she removed a silent scanner from her pack and pinged the area one hundred square feet in every direction. It seemed unlikely to her that Magrite's captors would have rigged high-end surveillance equipment in this public building, but the silence of the top floors of the research center had given her pause. Fortunately, the scan intercepted only the wireless signal of a laptop in the lab she was heading for, and a low band spike that probably indicated Magrite's guards were using some kind of walkie-talkie to stay in contact with one another.

Stowing her gear, Sydney began the uncomfortable crawl from one corner of the space to the other. She was careful to avoid contact with the insulation and pipes that crisscrossed the area, and equally careful to avoid the ceiling panels that covered wide squares of the area. Most of them were made of flimsy particle board and would not have begun to support her weight had she fallen onto them.

Her course took her in as much of an *L* shape as she could manage, given the obstacles. She was intentionally avoiding as much of the guarded hallway as she could. She didn't think she was making an unusual amount of noise, but there was no reason to get cocky.

Once she had reached the area directly above the room where she assumed she would find Magrite, she adjusted herself into a relatively comfortable crouched position and, with a flick of her thumb, opened one of her backpack's exterior pockets and removed a tube of lip balm. As she took a moment to rub a little on her lips, a pleasant memory from the day before flashed through her head.

"I know what you're thinking," Marshall had begun. "To the naked or uneducated eye this looks like lip balm." Removing the lid, Marshall took a moment to dab a little on his lips. He then rubbed them together, closed his eyes, and smiled faintly as he inhaled. "A fine blend of eucalyptus and mint," he continued. "Carrie's got me on this whole aromatherapy kick. Our bathroom, well you can't take a step without tripping over a candle or a basket of soothing salts. I don't know. I was pretty skeptical when she first suggested the kiwi cleansing extract, but I've got to tell you—"

He'd stopped himself there. Though he probably would have gone on, encouraged by the wide smile Sydney was doing her best to repress, had it not been for the look in Jack's eyes, which clearly indicated his lack of interest in any and all things aromatherapeutic.

"Anyway . . . screw off the top, soothe your lips. Unscrew the bottom, however," he said as he demonstrated, "and you've got a parabolic microphone embedded in the base."

"Nice," Sydney remembered acknowledging.

"But that's not all," Marshall had continued, as if he were selling them a new car. Handing the base that he had unscrewed back to Syd, Marshall had pointed out a slight indentation in the decorative pattern engraved on the tube. "Press here and . . . viola . . . self-injecting remote maneuverable wide-angle camera suitable for all your surveillance needs, especially in a tight space." Tossing a matching powder case to Syd, he added, "Of course you will have a remote-image feed going back to your operation center, but in addition this is a handy dandy monitor for your own personal use. Just be real gentle with that powder pad."

Sydney hadn't had to ask Marshall to replace the actual lip balm with a fresh one. After his demonstrations Marshall always did that as a matter of course. He'd been even more methodical and maniacal in his antigerm fastidiousness since Mitchell was born, and as she placed the balm on the ceiling a few feet from her position and adjusted the signal on her earpiece to carry the additional feed of the microphone along with her open signal to Jack, she decided that Carrie's new aromatherapy phase was a welcome one. The lip balm was both functional and refreshing.

She adjusted the volume and detected clearly the faint clicking below of fingers typing on a computer keyboard.

"Phoenix to Raptor, are you picking up the signal?" she whispered.

"Affirmative," Jack replied.

As she was considering just how long she might have to wait in this relatively uncomfortable position for anything regarding the identity of Magrite's captor to be revealed, she heard her father's voice, urgent in her ear. "Hold, Phoenix," Jack said sharply.

"What is it?" Syd asked, but seconds later didn't need the answer. In the distance the microphone was picking up the unmistakable rhythmic patter of several feet approaching the room. A few more moments, a grumbling acknowledgment that could have been a name or simply a "Yes sir," and Syd distinctly heard a loud *click* that indicated that the door had been unlocked and opened. At least three people entered the room.

The typing stopped.

"And how are we progressing, Arthur?" asked a rather soft, almost soothing voice with a thick Indian accent.

There was a pause, then Magrite's reply, "I've told you . . . this will take time."

"How much time?" the first voice asked with

just a hint of malice. There was a shuffling of feet. Someone had moved, probably closer to Magrite.

Sydney kept part of her concentration focused on the conversation below, but at the same time she reached for the engraved lid of the lip balm, found the indentation Marshall had shown her the day before, and pressed the nail of her index finger into it.

"This is complicated work," Magrite was saying. "It cannot be rushed. Even the slightest miscalculation . . ."

As delicately as she could, Sydney pressed the base of the lid into the ceiling panel to her immediate left, eighteen inches from the microphone she had already planted. Her earpiece cracked with the hiss and click that indicated Marshall's camera had now embedded itself in the panel.

"Yes, yes. You have my sympathies. But you understand that time is something we are sorely lacking."

Sydney reached for her backpack. Stowed in the same pocket where she had packed the lip balm was the compact case Marshall had given her. She was certain that her father was monitoring both the audio feed she had already established and the new video feed, but unless she could aim the camera toward Magrite and his captor, this was little more than an expensive waste of time.

"I am working as fast as I can," Magrite pleaded.

With an almost inaudible *click*, Sydney released the clasp on the compact and opened it. What would have been a four-by-two-inch mirror was actually a high-resolution plasma monitor, currently picking up the feed from the camera she had just activated. The black-and-white image on the screen was a crystal clear picture of the floor of the lab below. Two long workbenches filled the left side of the frame, stacked with several clear glass containers, Bunsen burners, and a utility sink. In the upper right-hand corner Sydney could barely make out the edge of what looked like a stool set against another high table.

Just be real gentle with that powder pad, she heard Marshall's voice remind her.

The half of the compact that was not devoted to the monitor looked exactly like a cake of face powder. Sydney placed her right index finger in the center of it, and gently moved her finger directly up. The image on the monitor immediately jumped. She now had a clear view of the far wall, several feet from the action she needed to see.

"I believe you," the voice of the captor said clearly. "But I wonder if you have been properly motivated."

"What do you mean?" There was a new edge to Magrite's voice. If Sydney had been able to see him, she thought it likely she would have watched the color drain from his face as he said it.

Gently moving her finger over the powder pad, which she discovered was only slightly more sensitive than a typical touch pad on a computer, she was able to focus the camera's lens on Magrite and the three men who had entered the room.

A short, stocky man in his early fifties with a full head of white hair that contrasted sharply with his deep brown skin seemed to be the group's leader. He was dressed in an expensive-looking tailored suit and silk tie. Sydney didn't recognize him, but her attention was drawn quickly from his face to the two men who stood a few feet behind him. Never mind what they were wearing. The semiautomatic rifles both were carrying made their job description perfectly clear.

Magrite had his back to the camera. He had risen from the stool where he had been working. A laptop computer lay open on the high table to his right.

White Hair had taken a pause before stepping even closer to Magrite to answer his question.

"I mean that despite the generous settlement which you have been promised—"

"I told you," Magrite shouted, "I don't want your money!"

White Hair continued as if the doctor hadn't spoken. "And despite our assurances that once you have succeeded, you will be released unharmed—"

"I don't give a damn what happens to me!" Magrite replied fiercely.

"Your failure to generate anything substantive has forced me to conclude that you are not serious about honoring your part of our agreement."

Sydney watched, analyzing every bit of data as this scene played out before her. Magrite had the temper and demeanor of a man who had been pushed well beyond his limits. Sydney wondered if the doctor was still physically and mentally capable of providing whatever his captor had demanded of him. In the pause that followed White Hair's last statement she saw Magrite's shoulders slump. The force of will that had sustained him in this brief exchange had abandoned him as quickly as it had come. Sydney had operated more than once on such sharp bursts of adrenaline. It was one of the body's most powerful drugs, but it had its limits. Something beyond the fear and long hours was tearing at Magrite. For the first time Sydney began to suspect that these people had something on Magrite of which APO was unaware.

"Please . . . you can't . . . ," Magrite was begging. At any moment, it seemed, he might just fall to his knees.

"Despite the fact that you seem determined to think only of yourself right now—"

"You know that's not true," Magrite interjected hopelessly.

"I have refrained from taking more aggressive and distasteful action."

This seemed to calm Magrite a bit. He staggered back to his stool, placing a hand there to steady himself.

"I swear to you, I am doing all that I can. Give me a few more hours."

"I am not unreasonable," White Hair replied. "But you are not the only one who will suffer if you fail, though it is my sincere hope that it will not come to that. I have tried to inspire you as best I can, but I believe you need to be reminded of the pain we will all feel if you do not provide me with the information I have requested."

With a nod to the gun-wielding thug on his left, the man with the white hair strode briskly toward the door. Thug number one wasted no time in crossing to Magrite, turning the butt of his gun on the doctor, and thrusting it into his gut.

Every humanitarian instinct in Sydney's body screamed for her to drop from her perch in the ceiling and put an end to this. Only the tactically trained portion of her brain made her resist. The two armed men in the room, she could probably handle. The problem was she wasn't sure if that left one guard, or the full complement of three guards still outside the door. Magrite couldn't be counted on to be a physical asset in the battle that was to come. He was weak, and now injured. It sounded like Magrite might be left alone in the next few minutes, assuming he survived them. Sydney believed that whatever these people wanted from Magrite, they wanted badly enough to let him live, at least a little longer. Unfortunately, the choice that gave her the highest odds of ultimate success necessitated that she remained still and watched as Magrite was further "inspired" by his brutal captors.

Magrite had fallen to the floor with the initial pummeling. Thug number one nodded to his accomplice, who then moved behind Magrite and pulled him up off the floor. As his partner held Magrite by the shoulders, the first man slung his weapon over his shoulder and spent the next few moments landing punch after punch on Magrite's face and in his stomach.

There was only so much Syd could reasonably take. She'd seen worse but never been able to make peace with such senseless violence. Syd was obviously capable of inflicting the same kind of pain as Magrite's two guards, and had done so time and time again in the line of duty. But she had only on the rarest of occasions enjoyed what she had to do. The two men brutally pummeling Magrite were taking altogether too much pleasure in their actions.

Given the tumult below, she felt safe signaling to Jack. Cupping her hand over her earpiece to eliminate any sound that might escape from it, she whispered, "Raptor, I'm going in."

"Wait!" was Jack's urgent response.

* * *

The moment Syd had activated the camera, Jack's visual monitor had clicked on, giving him sound and picture of the conversation between Magrite and his captors. He could imagine how Syd was taking this. She would have been anxious to enter the fray and put a stop to what she was witnessing. Sitting and watching would have filled her with a sense of uselessness, for which he knew she would have little patience.

He knew because in her place he would have felt exactly the same. And thirty years ago he, like Sydney, would have been tempted to throw caution to the wind and simply hurl himself into the battle. He counted among his life's regrets the few times he had acted on these poor choices, and heaven knew he didn't want Syd to accumulate any more regrets than were absolutely necessary.

Reluctant to risk exposing Syd, he had remained quiet while Magrite had been interrogated. Silently he had willed her to hold back until the road before her was both clearer and safer. This was not always a viable option, but Jack had read Magrite's situation immediately and was absolutely certain that if Syd would give them just a few more moments, the room would empty and she could extract Magrite with a minimum of danger.

While waiting for the room to clear, Jack had captured a still image of the white-haired man who was most likely responsible for Magrite's kidnapping, and uploaded it to the CIA's computerized identification program. He watched, tense, as hundreds of potential matches flashed across his screen until the computer found an image that matched, within a reasonable statistical probability.

It took less than forty seconds for the identification to come up. Jack compared the photos and was satisfied with the results. As he glanced over the man's background sheet, Jack realized with satisfaction that they'd just caught a serious break. He was 90 percent positive that the man who'd been talking to Magrite was not only the kidnapper but also the designer of the biological weapon they had come to identify.

The man in question was Surgit Gupta. He had recently been named to Proto-Chem's board of directors and had served for the last year as a vice president of development.

But that was just his day job.

Gupta had more than a dozen known aliases, all of them tied to various radical political movements and terrorist cells. He'd never been involved directly enough to warrant prosecution, but he'd amassed quite a fortune trading in illicit conventional weapons as far back as the early eighties.

It wasn't a huge leap to infer that his alliance with Proto-Chem was meant to cover his transition into the biological weapons market. He'd probably bought his legitimate cover with huge "donations" and been left to use one of the company's many foreign research centers for his own twisted ends.

But the operation in Kanpur was dark. The absence of bodies at the research center in question told Jack that Gupta had already completed his work on the Marburg strain. The only question still remaining was, Why had he kidnapped Magrite rather than killed him?

That critical piece of the puzzle still needed to find its place, and if Sydney entered the room too soon, she would expose their operation to Gupta. Until they knew Gupta's complete agenda, that wasn't the best move. A quiet extraction of Magrite would buy them the time they needed to pass the question on to the researchers at APO headquarters, and hopefully allow APO to remain one step ahead of Gupta.

"They're going to kill him if I don't get in there," Sydney growled through Jack's earpiece.

"No, they're not," he assured her. "I've identified the man holding Magrite as Surgit Gupta. He's a known terrorist and fully capable of developing the Marburg strain."

"That's great," Syd replied. "I'll get him, too."

"No!" Jack replied more forcefully. "Until we know why they wanted Magrite alive, we still won't understand Gupta's endgame. We need to get Magrite out of there without tipping Gupta off to the fact that we're after him."

There was a pause as Sydney considered this. He knew she'd grudgingly see the wisdom in this, and didn't push her further. Instead, Jack turned to the camera display and saw Magrite being tossed unceremoniously to the floor. The two armed men made their way toward the door.

"You're almost clear, Phoenix," Jack said.

The door had barely clicked shut when Sydney replied, "I'm going in."

"I'll meet you at the extraction point," Jack replied.

Jack secured his equipment, shutting down the live video and audio feed, and moved to the driver's seat of the van. Moments later he had turned off the side street where he'd been parked and made his way through the university's east gate. The research center had a large parking lot at the rear of the building. Jack pulled into a loading zone and waited for Sydney to emerge. They had briefly considered setting the pickup location off the grounds of the campus. Because neither of them had been able to predict Magrite's physical condition, should they find him, Jack had insisted on choosing the more dangerous but closer option of the parking lot. Given what they had just witnessed, it seemed a propitious choice. It was unlikely Magrite would walk out of that building. Syd would probably have to all but carry him.

Jack put the transmission in park and left the motor running, his eyes glued to the southeast staircase door. Sydney had closed her comm channel. Although he could initiate communication if he chose to, at the moment, he couldn't hear the blow by blow of Syd's rescue of Magrite.

He wasn't worried.

As the minutes ticked by and Sydney failed

to appear, he decided he might have relaxed a bit too soon.

SOWETO, SOUTH AFRICA

Cecilia Minden was apparently a fan of roses. The front yard and bricked path leading to the door of the small stucco home in Soweto's only "middle-class" suburb was packed with several hardy and fragrant varieties most suitable to the dry heat. Though Dixon didn't pause to admire them as he made his way toward the porch steps, he couldn't help but note, even in the waning light of dusk, that several of the plants might be hybrids Minden had developed herself.

In any part of the western world the narrow dirt road lined with modest dwellings would have denoted the least affluent of neighborhoods. Minden's home was exceptional in that the windows, all protected with solid glass panes, were also shuttered. A small air-conditioning unit hummed noisily from an opening that had been carved into the wall to the right of the front door.

Above the wooden front door, which was protected by two dead bolts, a pair of battery operated security lights should have illuminated the front porch the minute Dixon stepped within their sensor's range. He checked the lights with a slight twinge of alarm when they didn't automatically turn on, and realized that both of the bulbs had been smashed.

Vaughn waited in the truck they had rented in Johannesburg, keeping watch on the street and the home's exterior. The security lights were a bad sign, but Dixon refrained from calling for assistance.

There were no lights visible within the house. Dixon knocked once. Receiving no response, he hazarded a "Mrs. Minden" loud enough for the elderly woman to hear but not so obnoxious as to startle her neighbors.

Again, no response.

Reaching into his pocket for his lock-picking kit, he grasped the knob of the door with his free hand and felt it give instantly to the slight pressure he applied.

Trading the lock pick for a flashlight, and firmly grasping his 9mm with the other hand, Dixon slowly pushed the door open and called again, "Mrs. Minden . . . are you there?"

It was pitch black inside the house. The shuttered windows ensured that whatever faint light still stretched from the western horizon did not penetrate the home's interior.

Playing his flashlight over the entryway, he automatically looked for signs of a struggle. The small entry hall was furnished with only a large mirror on one wall, and a tall ceramic vase in the corner, which was filled with umbrellas and a few carved walking sticks.

British expatriates, Dixon recalled.

The first doorway to the right opened into a modest living room. An overstuffed couch and arm chair were placed around a low glass-topped cocktail table. An upright piano sat along the room's far wall, behind the sofa. A few unremarkable watercolors were framed on the walls and gave the room its only cheer.

Apart from the oppressive emptiness, nothing thus far seemed out of order.

Dixon passed the living room and continued toward the back of the house. A hallway turned to the left leading toward what Dixon assumed would be bedrooms. An arch directly ahead opened into the home's kitchen, where Dixon immediately caught sight of an icebox. Large butterfly magnets held several loose sheets of paper on the door of the fridge. Dixon paused over the pages, taking note of a few finger paintings that must have been the work of the Minden grandchildren. He was about to continue on when he realized that one of the pages was filled with large scrawled sets of numbers that looked like calculations of some kind. He studied them for a moment until he understood that they actually were notes about some of the hybrid flowers that adorned the front yard.

Interesting.

Dixon turned to his right and methodically worked the flashlight over the counter. The remains of food in the dish-filled sink almost accounted for the rancid stench that had begun to permeate his nostrils the moment he'd entered. Then again, he knew that smell. A low bar bisected the room beyond the kitchen, separating it from a small breakfast nook. Dixon noted a vase of wilting roses placed in the center of the linoleum-topped table.

Lowering his flashlight, he found what he had instinctively been seeking from the moment he'd entered the kitchen and his nose had registered the odor; a hint of pink puffy fabric on the floor of the nook. Passing a few steps farther into the kitchen, Dixon saw that the fabric was part of a house shoe, still on the foot of an elderly white woman.

He pressed on, moving to the edge of the divider until he had illuminated the entire body of what he assumed was Cecilia Minden, sprawled facedown on the floor, her arms tangled in the bottom-most rungs of one of the chairs. Dixon knelt beside her, examining every inch of the robe-clad frame until he could clearly see the matted white hair at the back of her skull that was tangled with dried blood.

Single shot to the back of the head.

Execution-style.

"Shotgun?"

"Go ahead, Outrigger."

"Call for a forensic unit . . . and get in here."

KANPUR, INDIA

Sydney didn't waste time packing her gear. The moment Jack cleared her for entry, she double-checked the plasma screen to confirm the room was empty, stowed it in her backpack, and removed the ceiling panel to her right. The floor of the lab was fourteen feet below. Holding one of the support beams with both hands, she dropped her legs through the opening, and once she was fully extended, she released her fingers and landed lightly on the floor.

The guards had been a little too enthusiastic in their beating of the doctor. Magrite was conscious, moaning and gasping for air as he cradled his stomach in a wounded fetal position. His attackers had probably broken his nose. There wasn't another head wound Sydney could see that would account for the blood pouring down his face.

He didn't sense her presence until she was crouched just in front of him. The moment he did, he flinched instinctively, but Sydney placed what she hoped was a gentle and reassuring hand on his arm, and said softly, "It's going to be okay, Dr. Magrite. I'm here to help you."

Magrite forced his eyes open and looked at Sydney with total confusion. She'd seen this face before on other people she'd been sent to rescue. He didn't seem to know whether he should be more or less afraid than he already was.

"Can you get up?" she asked.

Magrite coughed, choking on his own blood. He made no effort to rise.

"Please, Dr. Magrite, we don't have much time," Sydney said.

"Who . . . who . . . ?" Magrite gasped.

"That doesn't matter right now. I'm going to get you out of here," Sydney replied.

Magrite appeared to consider her offer.

Because he's had a better one? Sydney couldn't help but wonder.

Then Dr. Magrite did the last thing in the world Sydney had expected. Taking a deep breath, he screamed at the top of his lungs, "GUARDS! HELP ME! HELP!"

CHAPTER 6

SOWETO, SOUTH AFRICA

Dixon didn't wait for Vaughn's confirmation. Certain that his partner was doing as he'd requested, Dixon continued his search of the house. He now walked with his gun outstretched before him, his flashlight braced on the wrist of the hand that held the gun. His gut said the house was empty, probably had been for a couple of days. But you couldn't be too careful.

The first bedroom he came to had the welcoming but impersonal feel of a guest bedroom. A single daybed stretched along one wall. Another wall was covered floor to ceiling with bookcases, most of them overflowing with gardening references.

There were a few framed photos on the walls. Most were black-and-white images of a younger Cecilia Minden and a man Dixon assumed had been her husband, Theodore.

They were happy once, Dixon thought. *How did it come to this?*

Moving on to the second room off the hall, he decided this must have been Mrs. Minden's bedroom. A floral comforter was folded neatly at the base of a full-size bed. The bed filled the majority of the small room. An antique chest of drawers and a wooden rocking chair were the room's only other pieces of furniture.

The chest was dusty and covered with bric-a-brac. Porcelain figurines and a few strings of beads sat atop a lace runner that had once been white but was now yellowing with age. There were two more photos amid the clutter. One, an eight by ten wedding portrait, showed a smiling young blond bride and her rather serious-looking groom. The other, the only recent picture he'd found so far, was an image of Cecilia and a young girl, perhaps six or seven years old.

The little girl was smiling shyly. Short wiry black curls poked out from under a pink-and-red scarf. Her coloring was that of a fair-skinned African, but her eyes were a piercing blue.

Despite the broad smile on Cecilia's face, Dixon doubted that this little girl was a relative. If Cecilia had recently adopted a local child, he believed their records would have shown that. But the dresser seemed to display only treasured possessions.

A tight rope of worry pulled itself taut around Dixon's chest.

The watercolors on the refrigerator.

If that little girl lived in this house . . .

Dixon quickly scanned the rest of the room and returned to the hallway. Apart from an empty bathroom on his right, there was only one door left. It stood ominously closed at the end of the hall.

The door creaked in protest as Dixon pushed it gently open. Tensing with fear, Dixon took in the furnishings in a glance. The floor was cluttered with toys, dolls, games, blocks, and books. A small table with two chairs in one corner was set for a tea party. A stuffed rabbit placed in one of the chairs waited for his hostess to return.

A school desk stood against the wall to Dixon's right. Atop it sat a new computer. The Barbie screen saver gave the room its only illumination apart from Dixon's flashlight.

To his left, tucked into the corner, was a small bed. It was youth-size, smaller than a standard twin and lower to the ground. A carved headboard and footboard bracketed the thin mattress. Dixon's daughter, Robin, had slept in such a bed until her eighth birthday, when she had announced to Dixon and his wife, Diane, that she was much too old for a little-girl bed and Winnie-the-Pooh sheets. It had broken his heart to take that bed down and replace it with his daughter's "big-girl" bed. As far as he was concerned, she could stay little forever.

A brightly colored woven blanket was tossed across a good-size lump in the center of the bed. A white teddy bear sat at the foot of the bed, its plastic black eyes accusing Dixon of arriving too late. It was difficult to tell from the doorway what might be under that blanket, and much as Dixon didn't really want to find out, he moved cautiously toward it.

He thought of the picture, Cecilia and the unidentified little girl. If what he feared as he approached the bed was true, maybe it was a blessing that Cecilia had not lived to see it. He kept seeing Robin and his son, Steven, in his mind's eye. Several months ago they'd been kidnapped by the Covenant, which wanted to force Dixon to retrieve a Rambaldi artifact housed at Operation Black Hole, in exchange for the children's safe return. The paralyzing shock and terror of those few days would never leave him. Though both children had survived the ordeal, Dixon had refused to take one moment for granted since then. His children were the most precious gift this life had given him. He had managed to work through so many losses—the loss of his identity when SD-6 had been revealed as a sham, the loss of his beloved Diane. Enduring the pain of those events had changed him. But he had not grown so hard nor so cold that the potential loss of his children did not fill him with a scorching sick dread. He knew, of course, that his children were safe and sound in Los Angeles at this very moment. He'd said good morning to them via satellite phone just a few hours earlier while en route to Soweto. Yet as he approached the little bed and grasped the blanket to uncover whatever lay beneath, he burned and ached with anger that this could happen to anyone's child.

The rush of relief that coursed through him was released in an audible sigh when the blanket was pulled back to reveal nothing but two pillows. Shaking off the horror of his own fears, he returned his attention to the room and began to scan it more thoroughly.

From the front door he heard Vaughn entering.

"Dixon!" he called.

"Back here," Dixon replied.

Dixon turned his attention to the computer. For the first time he realized that on top of it rested another photo. The frame that housed it was carved wood. Block letters ran along the right side, spelling out the word "Daddy."

The photo was of the little girl he had already seen, but this image had captured her mid-laugh and at least four or five years older, sitting on the knee of a man Dixon did not immediately recognize.

Grasping the frame, he brought the face directly under his flashlight and studied it briefly. It didn't take long for him to realize why he hadn't identified the man right away. The man in the photo, like the girl, was smiling broadly, and Dixon had never seen an image of this man that showed him happy.

The man in the photo, the little girl's daddy, was Dr. Arthur Magrite.

KANPUR, INDIA

Am I missing something? Syd had a split second to wonder, even as her reflexes took control of her body and she moved in a swift fluid motion from Magrite's side to the door through which at any moment his guards were sure to enter.

One minute they're beating the crap out of him, and the next . . . he wants their help?

Before she had time to give it more thought, the door burst open and one of the guards strolled in casually, asking, "You want more, old man?"

One of Sydney's greatest strengths in the field was her uncanny ability to use to her advantage whatever was handy. In this case that was the heavy metal door. Grasping it with both hands, she shoved it hard into the man who had just entered. His head thwacked against it with a satisfying *thud* before the forward momentum plunged him to the ground. Syd rushed to plant one foot on the hand that had sprawled in the direction of the rifle, which had flown from the guard's hands as he fell. She heard the bones of the hand crack. With her free foot she kicked the rifle well out of range under one of the lab tables.

Guard number two had decided to show some interest in the doctor's call only when he caught a glimpse of his partner being pummeled to the floor. Rather than entering the room with his rifle pointed right in front of him, he charged in holding it across his body. Sydney met him head-on, grasping the semiautomatic with both hands and raising it to his face to punch him with the side of the barrel. A solid knee to the groin sent him reeling back into the hallway. Syd took a quick leap to her right and grabbed the bench Magrite had been working on, holding it before her with the long blunt legs jutting out.

Guard number three knew enough by now to enter the room with his gun pointed in the right direction. Sydney rammed him from the side with the stool, tangling the gun and his arms in the long legs, and forcing him off balance.

By this time the guard with one remaining good hand was on his feet again. Syd engaged him hand to hand, landing a solid punch to his stomach and following it with a high kick to the face. He blocked it automatically with his bad hand,

and Syd noted with some satisfaction that he withered a bit with the pain. She would have finished him right there if guard number two hadn't been rushing back into the room, also holding his gun pointed directly at them. Syd grabbed the first guard and used his body as a shield to take the three quick shots, which pelted into his back.

One down, two to go.

As the fight began, Magrite managed to pull himself halfway up and lean against the base of the lab table. His breath was coming back to him, though the pain radiating down his neck, and the shock of sensation that accompanied any motion in his right shoulder, threatened to send him rapidly into the dark waters of unconsciousness.

Just keep breathing. In and out.

The woman who had come to rescue him was amazing. He didn't know what he had expected her to do when he'd called for the guards. Probably just retreat to wherever she had come from. There was only one door to the room where he'd been held for the past two days. He knew she hadn't entered that way. As best he could tell she had materialized out of thin air. But whatever her origins, the word "retreat" was obviously not part of her vocabulary.

He watched as with efficient brutality she met and subdued the first attacks presented by all three of the armed men, each of whom had several inches and at least forty pounds on her. Not to mention the fact that they were armed and she did not appear to have a weapon on her.

Maybe she didn't need one. *Maybe she is a weapon.*

By the time she had managed to position herself behind the body of the first man and force him into the line of his companion's fire, Magrite had begun to realize that the competition playing out before him was by no means an assured victory for either side. The two men who remained were both armed, and should have been able to easily subdue her. But that wasn't happening.

His call for help had been a gut reaction. It wasn't that he didn't want to leave. He couldn't. It was simply not an option. Only now did it occur to him to wonder if whoever had come to his aid also knew about Katelyn. Perhaps she was already safe. Perhaps this stranger fighting for his life should have been given the benefit of the doubt.

No. It was a chance he simply could not take.

Surely he had done the right thing. But as the battle continued to turn in her favor, he realized he was moments away from another choice, a choice he hated to make without more information. But he had to know who to trust. For now the only person who held power over him was Gupta, and until Magrite knew that power was removed from Gupta's hands, he would not risk putting his daughter in further danger. He had never imagined that she would not be safe in Cecilia's care. How had Gupta even managed to discover her identity and location? It was a secret he had never betrayed, even to his few close friends.

Katelyn had always and would always come first. He owed her that much. *He owed her everything.*

Turning his head painfully to the right, he saw the strap of the gun the woman had kicked from the hand of her first attacker. As quickly as his pain would allow he used his left hand to pull his body beneath the table until the gun was within reach.

No one else in the room was paying him any attention. A few seconds more and they would have no choice.

Ignoring the spasm of agony that racked his

shoulder, he held himself steady with his left hand and reached out with his right to grasp the base of the gun. He allowed himself a few seconds of gasping relief after he had pulled it to his chest. Clutching it in his weaker right arm, he then reached up with his left to grab the top of the worktable and pull himself up on shaking legs.

He had never fired a weapon of any kind before. Only for his daughter would he ever have dared attempt it.

The death of his companion didn't seem to give the attacker pause. As professional as these men were, Sydney hadn't thought it would. Ignoring the shock now permanently etched on the face of the dying man, and the blood that had begun to trickle from his mouth, she shifted her weight back on her left leg and used the added momentum of his weight to send him soaring into the body of his killer.

From the corner of her left eye she caught sight of the man she had momentarily trapped with the stool. He had disentangled himself and was climbing over the wreckage of the lab tables and empty chairs he had fallen into, raising his gun to fire directly at her. She wheeled out of his way before he had a chance to aim properly, grabbing the broken leg of a wooden chair as she did so. Before he had a chance to regroup, she had positioned herself beside him, bringing the chair leg down with the force of both hands, forcing the gun out of his grasp. She then knocked him squarely on the back of the head with the blunt end of the leg. Unfortunately, this didn't send him plummeting to the ground as she had anticipated. If anything it only seemed to make him angrier.

He roared with the pain, stumbling forward into the only remaining clear floor space in the center of the room, and steadying himself to face her again.

Sydney didn't hesitate. She rushed forward, landed a spin-kick to his torso, and ducked under the right hook he sent to answer it. As she recovered, he managed to send a solid punch with his left into the side of Sydney's face. Had the full force of his body weight been behind it, it would have knocked her out cold. But the impact was more bracing than incapacitating. Sydney ducked again, moving closer and landing four quick jabs to his gut. As he backed up under their force, she pinned his left foot to the floor under her left foot and, moving past him diagonally, kicked his knee from the side with enough force to bend it inward, shattering the joint.

He fell to the ground, in obvious agony. Sydney didn't spare a moment of sympathy. She finished him with a solid downward kick to the back of the head. He might survive when he woke up. But it would be a while, and a headache he would never forget.

The few seconds she had spent engaging this one man had given the shooter time to disentangle himself from his dead companion and reenter the fray. He had probably been watching for a clean shot for less than three seconds when Sydney finished off the second guard. Nonetheless, the moment he went down, he squared his weapon directly at Sydney.

At that very moment both he and Sydney were forced to pause by the sound and tone of Dr. Magrite's voice as he shouted, "Shoot her and you die!"

Sydney spared a glance at Magrite, who was now standing at the point of the triangle formed by all three of them. Magrite was holding one of the semiautomatics and pointing it directly at the guard who had made the incalculable error of listening to him, rather then following through and shooting Sydney.

So whose side is he on now? Sydney wondered.

"Drop the gun!" the guard shouted automatically.

Yeah, that'll work.

Magrite was shaking but his voice never wavered.

"Shut up!" Magrite replied. "You," he said next, nodding to Sydney. "Just tell me . . . is she safe?"

Sydney had no clue who "she" was, but her gut told her that a well-intentioned lie was the way to go at this point. Once there were two fewer guns loaded and aimed, there would be time for a more reasoned discussion.

"Of course," she replied.

A faint, fatalistic smile crossed Magrite's lips, and he focused his attention again on the guard.

Just as Sydney did, the guard must have realized Magrite's intentions almost immediately. Sydney didn't really care if Magrite finished off his last captor for her. The problem was that by telegraphing his intentions so broadly he had just doomed himself.

It all played out in slow motion. The guard

sensed Magrite's next move, and his trigger finger responded automatically.

Magrite had obviously never shot anyone. Sydney caught the split second of hesitation in his eyes as the guard was reacting, and she knew that now Magrite wasn't ever going to get a chance to. This was one reality of the human psyche every single field agent who had fired a weapon in the line of duty understood, but that Magrite had probably never considered when he'd picked up that weapon. Killing another human being, even in self-defense, was an unnatural act, unless you were a sociopath. The best-trained individual, let alone a complete novice, would take an extra second or two before pulling the trigger for the first time. Oftentimes that second meant the difference between life and death. You had to be prepared for it . . . know it would be there . . . and with superhuman will force yourself beyond it to survive your first confrontation. Magrite had no such preparation. Despite his intention to kill the guard, he hesitated ever so briefly as the full awareness of what he was about to do rained down on him.

That hesitation was all it took.

The guard did not pause.

Knowing the futility of what she had to do, Sydney nevertheless rallied her senses and leaped into the air, throwing herself at the armed guard as he fired shot after shot toward Magrite.

The guard didn't have time to counter Sydney's attack. He got off four clean rounds before he was on the ground beneath her. She immediately grabbed the semiautomatic and brought the butt of it down into the center of his face, crushing the front of his skull.

Panting, and splattered with the blood of at least two of the three men she had just fought, Sydney rose and turned to Magrite.

He was lying on his back, one arm folded over his chest, the other splayed out to his side. He coughed with a couple of quick breaths. Each time his chest contracted with an exhalation, small fountains of blood were forced upward from the three gaping wounds in his chest.

Oh, no, Sydney thought.

The man she had been sent to extract had only a few brief moments of life left to him.

SOWETO, SOUTH AFRICA

Vaughn found Dixon in the back bedroom of the Minden house, standing before a small desk and holding a framed photograph. Dixon looked up sharply as he entered.

"Take a look," he said, handing the photo to Michael.

It didn't take Vaughn long to put the pieces together.

"Magrite has a daughter?" he asked. "Kind of an important piece of information, don't you think? Why didn't we know about it?"

"I don't know, but I guess this explains the regular payments Magrite was sending to Minden," Dixon offered.

Glancing around the little girl's room, Michael hesitated, then asked, "Have you found her body?"

Dixon shook his head.

"So where is she?" Vaughn asked rhetorically.

As he set the photo down on the desk next to a hot-pink mouse pad, he inadvertently deactivated the monitor's screen saver. The smiling face of Barbie vanished in a shower of pixels and was replaced by a standard desktop, scattered with icons.

Vaughn glanced at them. Most were colorful little images with names such as Ultimate Fantasy Puzzles or Barbie's Design Studio. He was about to turn his attention elsewhere when Dixon said, "What are those?"

Vaughn looked back at the monitor. In the upper right-hand corner of the desktop were icons of standard yellow file folders. Beneath each folder was a name. The next breath he took caught in his chest when he saw that one of the names was Sowalzi.

Michael removed a pair of latex gloves from his pocket and snapped them on. He reached for the mouse and clicked Sowalzi's folder open.

Immediately a database form appeared before him. The main part of the screen was black, with prompts at the bottom such as RUN CODE and DISPLAY GENE. To the right of this work area was an active simulation of a strand of DNA. It twisted and turned, displaying a number of sections, each presented in a different color. Overlapping this image was a menu box that read SEQUENCE COMPLETE. SIMULATE CHANGES?

Michael didn't know enough about what he was looking at to feel totally comfortable playing around; it was obviously a highly sophisticated program. He did take a moment to move the cursor onto the image of the DNA strand, and he noted that as the cursor crossed a purple field that represented part of the strand, a series of letters began to run down the black screen beside it. There were only four letters: *A, T, C,* and *G.* Pairs of *A*s and *T*s lined up against pairs of *C*s and *G*s in no particular order, repeating over and over again until the screen was filled and automatically scrolling down to add data to the field.

Michael moved the mouse away from the image of the double helix, and the letter pairs disappeared.

"Marshall might just kiss one of us when we transmit this to him," Vaughn said.

"He can kiss you," Dixon replied. "My question is, What the hell is it doing here? Why would Magrite keep a program like this on his daughter's computer, instead of wherever he was working?"

"Maybe it's a backup," Michael suggested, not terribly convincingly.

"Hang on," Dixon said, pointing to a box on the bottom menu bar, which was labeled VECTOR MAP. "Click there."

Michael complied, and the black screen was suddenly filled with advanced calculations that included some of the A-T and C-G pairs. In addition, graphic representations of genes in various shades of blue were cross-referenced onto a separate DNA helix.

"None of this was in the hard copies of Magrite's files," Dixon announced, puzzled. "If this is the program he used to design the specific treatment protocol for each of his patients, why isn't this documentation part of his files?"

"I don't know," Vaughn replied. "But Marshall will."

He closed the program as Dixon began to scrutinize the room more carefully. There was a small craft table next to the computer desk, and it was stacked haphazardly with several childish drawings that were among jars of crayons and markers and palettes of well-used watercolors. Dixon sifted through the more impressionistic of them until he found a few drawings near the bottom that were clearly meant to be paintings of flowers. Roses.

Each flower had distinct color patterns. Below some of them were mathematical equations done in an awkwardly scrawled handwriting.

"I saw this same writing on some of the drawings attached to the refrigerator," Dixon said softly.

Turning the page over, they both saw that the drawing had been signed by the same hand. He passed the drawing to Vaughn.

"Katelyn Magrite, age eight," Vaughn read aloud.

Vaughn turned the drawing over and studied the equations more carefully. They were well beyond basic math. They were well beyond high school math.

"This isn't possible," he said.

"No, it isn't," Dixon agreed.

Vaughn glanced around the room again, then picked up the picture of Katelyn and Magrite and studied it more carefully. "She can't be more than ten, maybe eleven years old," he said.

"I know," Dixon answered in a way that suggested that the same impossible yet undeniable hypothesis had occurred to both of them.

"So she was doing algebra when she was eight?" was Vaughn's next question.

Dixon studied the calculations more closely. "Not just algebra. I think these figures represent theoretical hybrid potentials . . . for the roses. . . .

It had to be Magrite. He's a molecular biologist. He was toying around, doodling on his daughter's artwork," Dixon said, trying to convince himself, though the handwriting told another story.

"Sure," Vaughn replied. "I'm sure you did the same thing when Steven and Robin brought their finger paintings home from school."

They exchanged a glance. Of course Dixon hadn't, and both of them knew it. But the alternative was just too hard to even consider.

"She's not here," Dixon said, changing the subject. "We could assume she was also kidnapped. They had to know that in order to get to her they'd have to kill Minden. What would make all this worthwhile?"

"She's leverage," Michael concluded. "Whatever the kidnappers want Magrite to do, they took the little girl to make sure he agreed to do it."

"We have to find her," Dixon replied firmly. "They killed Cecilia Minden without mercy. They might have spared the little girl for the moment, to use her against Magrite, but the minute she becomes unnecessary . . ." He let the thought trail off.

"I know," Vaughn replied.

Dixon pulled out his secured satellite phone and patched a call through to APO headquarters. A few seconds later he said, "Get me Sloane. And tell Marshall we have another transmission for him."

KANPUR, INDIA

Sydney knelt at Magrite's side. The short gasps bursting from his rapidly failing respiratory system were coming more quickly with each few seconds.

Oh, God.

His injuries were every bit as bad as they'd looked from across the room. One shot had landed squarely in his gut. Pools of deep crimson were collecting in the folds of fabric that surrounded the wound. Had this been the only shot that had made contact, Magrite might have had a chance. The blood loss could be contained with pressure, which Sydney immediately began to apply with both hands. It was the other two shots that had sealed the deal. Both had penetrated his right torso, only a few inches a part. The gurgling and wheezing that accompanied the spurts of blood that shot from the holes with each gasp indicated that at least one of Magrite's lungs had collapsed.

Magrite was struggling to speak.

Maintaining the pressure on his gut as best she could, Sydney lowered her face to his to reduce the effort he would have to expend.

At first she could make no sense of the partial syllables interspersed with wet coughs. Finally, though, he seemed to settle on one sound she could almost make out.

"Kay . . . Kay . . . ," he said over and over.

"I'm sorry, Dr. Magrite," Sydney said softly. "I don't understand."

"Kay . . . Kay . . . Katelyn," he finally managed to gasp.

Who?

Then it dawned on Sydney: Whomever Magrite had been talking about when he'd asked if "she" was safe, was most likely Katelyn.

Magrite's biographical information had not included any mention of a significant other. Girlfriend, perhaps?

Not likely.

But there hadn't been mention of any immediate family either. He'd never been married. Both of his parents were deceased.

Unless . . .

Magrite's actions ever since he had called for the

guards suddenly made horrible and depressing sense. He had wanted to escape. That much she knew. But the other person who would suffer if he didn't give Gupta what he wanted, had to be Katelyn. He'd refused to be rescued because he was afraid for Katelyn's life. He had only chosen to trust Sydney when she lied and told him that "she" was safe.

True, there were a few people in Sydney's life whom she would have willingly laid her life down for in the line of duty. Vaughn and Dixon came immediately to mind. She knew they would have reciprocated. But Magrite's reckless behavior in the last fifteen minutes didn't resonate in the same place. His commitment to Katelyn went beyond what any normal person would feel for a close friend or lover. The desperation in Magrite's eyes when he had pleaded with her to tell him if she was safe, the strength that seemed to leave his body when Gupta had suggested that Magrite was thinking only of himself . . . those feelings came from a different place in the human heart and spirit.

She'd seen it before, in the eyes of her father. On the handful of occasions when her life had been in serious danger and he'd been powerless to come to her aid.

His daughter.

Magrite had less than a minute to live. It would have been kinder to perpetuate the lie . . . to let him die certain that Katelyn was safe. But she obviously wasn't. If Gupta had her, she needed Sydney's help now, more than Magrite did.

"Dr. Magrite," Sydney said softly, "Katelyn isn't safe. I have to get to her. Do you have any idea where they are holding her? I promise I won't rest until she's safe, but you have to help me."

Magrite choked back a spasm of anguish. With his last burst of strength he reached for Sydney with his left hand and clumsily grasped for her arm. She maintained the pressure on his abdomen with one palm, but raised the other hand to clasp his.

"They . . . don't . . . know," he struggled to say.

"What?" Sydney asked quickly. "What don't they know?"

Magrite took as deep a breath as his one functioning lung would allow, and with grim determination replied, "She was the one . . . not me." Tightening his hold like a vise on Sydney's hand, he made his last request. "They . . . must . . . *never* . . . know."

His voice trailed off with his final words. The pressure on Sydney's hand went slack as Magrite's eyes fixed themselves on a point in the distance and the painful rasps of his breath were silenced.

She was the one?

It didn't make any sense. But Sydney didn't have the luxury of time to figure it out right now. She left Magrite where he had fallen, and drenched in the blood of three dead men, she raced from the lab toward the extraction point where her father was waiting, without a thought for the backpack full of gear she'd left in the ceiling above the lab.

CHAPTER 7

SOWETO, SOUTH AFRICA

Less than an hour after Dixon and Vaughn's arrival, the interior and exterior of Cecilia Minden's home were ablaze in artificial light. The forensic team that had descended on the residence like a small army had come with their own power-supply van. Although the sun had set and it was now pitch black outside, the dozen or so halogen lamps set on tripods in the yard and in each of the home's small rooms gave the impression that within the perimeter of the Minden home, it was high noon.

The controlled chaos of a high-priority investigation always drew onlookers. Three agents had been posted in the front and rear yards to discourage the curious. Once the contents of Katelyn Magrite's computer had been transmitted to Marshall, the house had been turned over to the forensic analysts, and a small contingent of local police had been sufficiently encouraged to remain out of the way until the analysts' work was complete. Dixon had then scanned the gathering crowd for other pertinent sources of information.

The most promising were two women, also Brits like Minden, who had been her neighbors for almost fifteen years. Evangeline Rhodes and Grace Patterson were in their midsixties and shared Cecilia's love for gardening. Their small frame house was a riot of fragrant blooms, which Dixon admired as he was ushered into their sitting room and offered a cup of very weak tea.

"You're absolutely certain that nothing has happened to dear Katie?" Grace called from the kitchen, her voice tinged with fear.

"Katelyn wasn't in the house when we found Mrs. Minden," Dixon reassured her firmly.

"I told you something was wrong," Evangeline,

or Angel, as she preferred to be called, admonished Grace, who was fumbling with a plate of hurriedly assembled biscuits.

"When was the last time either of you saw Cecilia Minden, Ms. Rhodes?" Dixon asked, accepting a butter cookie.

"It was . . . ," Grace began.

"Thursday night last," Angel finished for her.

Angel was the hardier of the two, Grace the more reserved. Both had allowed their hair to grow in silver and white, though Angel's was close cropped just below her ears while Grace's longer locks were pinned back in a hurried bun, leaving several long curled wisps framing her fine delicate features. They shared the ease and tendency to overlap each other's thoughts that was common in any two people who had shared the majority of their lives with each other.

"I stopped over to borrow a fresh lemon for the herring," Angel continued.

"I couldn't make it to the market. My left hip—arthritis, you know—was acting up," Grace added apologetically.

"He doesn't care about your medical history, love." Angel gently cut her off before adding,

"Everything was fine. She'd just put Katie to bed and was going to do a little reading—"

"But Arthur . . . ," Grace interrupted.

"Yes," Angel acknowledged. "She mentioned she was worried about Arthur—Dr. Arthur Magrite, Katelyn's father. Do you . . . ?" She paused, momentarily uncertain.

Dixon nodded, understanding that they had reached the point in the interview where he was required to be as forthcoming as possible. Neither of these women were legally compelled to share any information with him. For the moment it seemed best to keep things polite.

"We know that Dr. Magrite was an old friend of the Mindens and that Mrs. Minden was caring for his daughter," he said, hoping that would be enough to keep them going.

"And you are with the American government?" Grace asked hesitantly.

"Yes, ma'am," Dixon replied.

"He's CIA, dearest," Angel said simply, as if she were commenting on nothing more serious than the weather, "or perhaps FBI. At any rate, you can be sure his employers are known only by their initials."

Grace's eyes grew wide and a little awestruck

as Angel took a moment to enjoy her little revelation. Dixon hadn't introduced himself as attached to any particular authority when he had first spoken to the two women. He had simply begun questioning them casually, before being told that if they were going to talk, they'd do it like civilized people, over a cup of tea.

Dixon nodded to Angel, without offering to clarify his position. For her part Angel didn't seem to require further information. She simply added, "I don't mean to be presumptuous, Mr. Dixon, but I've lived in Africa for twenty years. The local police couldn't scrounge up a bicycle thief if he walked into their offices and confessed. The resources you have brought to bear on our little street in the past hour alone gave you away. What I'm curious to know is why your government has taken such an interest in the affairs of a woman like Cecilia. Her death is certainly shocking, and tragic, but you and I both know it won't be in the morning papers across the pond."

"Unfortunately, the less I say at this point, the safer you'll both be," Dixon replied. "I know it must be frustrating to you both, but as I said before, anything you can tell me about your neighbor will aid our investigation and be much appreciated."

Angel considered Dixon appraisingly for a moment, then, apparently satisfied, continued. "Arthur and poor Teddy—Cecilia's husband—worked together in Johannesburg. For years Arthur was their third wheel, always stopping in for tea and holidays. Unfortunately, Teddy passed away quite suddenly—"

"Heart attack," Grace interjected.

"Yes, just a few years after we moved in. Cecilia was devastated, of course. And for some time after that we didn't see as much of Arthur. When he showed up at Cecilia's door almost eleven years ago with Katelyn, I thought she should have told him to sod off."

"Oh, Angel . . . no," Grace admonished.

"Now, of course, I'm glad she didn't. Katie is a special girl, and she needed the kind of care that only a woman with a heart like Cecilia's could provide."

"What do you mean 'special'?" Dixon asked.

"She is of mixed races, of course," Angel said simply. "Arthur never told Cecilia who the mother was, most likely one of those nurses he couldn't keep his hands off of. All he ever said was that Katie's mother had died in childbirth and there was no one else to care for the girl."

"Did you believe that was true?" Dixon asked.

"Oh, most likely," Angel replied. "Arthur is many things of which I do not approve, but he isn't a liar."

"He is a great man," Grace said approvingly.

"Yes," Angel agreed, "but like many 'great men' tends to remain focused only on those things that interest him."

"Now, you know he loves little Katie," Grace said.

"Of course, but he couldn't be bothered to stop in more than a few times a year before the accident."

"The accident?" Dixon asked.

"Katelyn always had a hard time with other children," Angel replied. "It was to be expected. Neither white nor black, no group was going to willingly accept her. And she was painfully shy, growing up. She and Cecilia sort of created their own little world together, but the child had to go to school, and when Cecilia entered Katie in the local kindergarten, I'm afraid, despite everyone's best efforts, Katelyn found few friends."

"Those boys were monsters," Grace said defiantly.

"Of course they were, love, but they were little boys. They couldn't have been expected to know better. They chased poor Katie up a tree. Odd thing really, for a child so shy to be so athletic. Perhaps she learned to run so fast and climb so high because she got used to being chased at such a young age. At any rate, she fell out of a tree on the school playground and was quite seriously injured."

"Something in her brain, poor dear." Grace shook her head sadly.

"Arthur did take her away briefly then. I'd heard he took her all the way back to Ontario. They saw all manner of specialists, and finally there was nothing more to be done, and so they returned and Cecilia took Katie in again."

"But after that, Arthur did come by much more regularly," Grace said in an obvious attempt to mitigate Angel's recitation of his past faults.

"He did. I'll give him that," Angel said.

"And he's here most nights the last year or so," Grace added.

"Has Arthur been contacted?" Angel suddenly asked sharply.

"We are doing our best to reach him right now," Dixon replied honestly.

"And what will happen to poor Katie?" Grace asked worriedly. "You don't think she saw—" A look of pure horror flashed across her flushing face.

"We don't know if she witnessed anything," Dixon replied as soothingly as possible. "Is there anywhere she might have gone, if she was afraid?"

"She would have come here. We're the closest thing to her only other family," Angel replied. "Grace and I were in town on Monday. I haven't seen either of them since then, but that's only been two days, and I'm certain that if Katelyn were frightened or worried . . . if she knew what had happened to Cecilia, she would have been here in a flash."

Dixon took this in. True, he'd never really believed that Katelyn had been anything but kidnapped. Angel's words only confirmed his worst fears and tightened the knot of tension settled in the pit of his stomach.

"Oh, dear," Grace fretted. "If anything has happened to that precious little girl, I'll never forgive myself."

"We'll find her, Ms. Patterson," Dixon said with a great deal more confidence than he felt. "Is there anything else you can tell me that might be useful?"

Angel paused, then added, "Just that . . . after the accident Katelyn was never the same. She was never quite . . . right . . . if you understand my meaning."

"Oh, hush Angel."

"I'm afraid I don't," Dixon replied.

"Cecilia tried to send her back to school. They haven't any kind of special education here, but Cecilia wanted her to be as normal as possible and to interact with children her own age. I quite agreed that growing up in a nest of mother hens like the three of us could be a daunting prospect for the girl, but when Katelyn came home with those new words . . ." She trailed off. For the first time a spasm of pain crossed her face. Her bright blue eyes caught fire as she continued. "They called her '*dutuwende*.' Do you know that word, Mr. Dixon?"

"I'm afraid I don't," he replied.

"It's local slang, a derogatory term, something akin to calling her stupid or retarded, I'm afraid."

"Did Katelyn suffer some kind of permanent brain damage in the accident?" Dixon asked.

"Of course," Angel said. "But you'd have to really know her to see it. There were areas where she was just a little slower than a normal child. She didn't speak clearly for a long time after."

"Oh, but she was getting so much better," Grace added.

"She was." Angel nodded. "Really her problem is just that she was so quiet. Sometimes I'd look at her. She'd get the strangest expressions on her face. Like she was listening to a song that none of us could hear, or watching a picture show in her head. She was quite herself around us, but that was to be expected. And after Cecilia took her out of school and started to teach her at home, Cecilia often commented on her brilliance with math."

"Oh, tell him about the roses," Grace suggested.

"Well, I think Cecilia was making far too much of it, but Katie took an interest in the garden and started helping with the rose plantings. Cecilia liked hybrids, always wanted to create a 'Minden' rose. She said that her first efforts with Katelyn were some of the most beautiful and strong she'd ever produced. But Katie was just a little girl. She couldn't possibly have understood. I think that was one of the many ways Cecilia liked to encourage her."

Dixon nodded, thoughtful.

Joshua Grey. It's rare, but possible.

"Thank you both," he finally said. "If I think of any other questions . . ."

"You'll be sure and stop by for tea?" Grace asked sweetly.

"I will. You've been very helpful."

Dixon drained his cup and rose to go. As he was

ushered out the front door, Angel caught his arm out of Grace's sight, and said softly, "Katelyn's dead too, isn't she? You understand it's not vile curiosity. It will break my poor darling's heart, and I would like to soften the blow."

Dixon took Angel's hand and held it firmly. "At this point I have no reason to believe she is. In fact, I honestly think that Katelyn is still very much alive."

"Then find her, won't you?" Angel asked.

"I'll do my best," Dixon replied.

"And tell whomever it is you need to tell that if Arthur doesn't want to take care of the child on his own, now that dear Cecilia is gone, Grace and I will be happy to stand in for her." Angel's lip quivered visibly before she added, "I know what it is to be alone in the world, Mr. Dixon. I wouldn't wish that on anyone, and despite his recent interest I don't know that Arthur can be depended upon long-term to really look after Katelyn."

"I'll keep that in mind," Dixon said, shaking her hand firmly.

As he crossed the yard on his way back to the Minden house, he turned the second most important piece of new information he'd gleaned from the interview over and over in his head.

Despite his recent interest, Angel had said.

What the hell had made Magrite so damned interested in the welfare of a child he'd dumped on an old friend and hardly bothered to visit for the first five years of her life? Maybe the accident had awakened some sense of parental responsibility. But Dixon had known too many men like Magrite—brilliant, but single-minded in the pursuit of their own ends. The halls of the intelligence community were littered with them; stars in their respective fields who had left shattered families in their wake. Something had changed fairly recently, something that made Katelyn more useful to him, if Dixon's gut was right.

He had a theory. But he wouldn't be able to confirm it without Marshall.

"Dixon!" Vaughn's call interrupted his musings.

"What is it?" he asked, rushing to his partner's side near the open door of their truck.

"Marshall's coming on the line," Vaughn replied. "You've got to hear this."

Dixon didn't doubt it.

KANPUR, INDIA: CIA SAFE HOUSE

Jack and Sydney had been forced to make an unplanned stop at the tenement in downtown

Kanpur that was held by the CIA in the name of Avril Singh. Little more than a studio apartment, it at least provided access to the shower that Syd desperately needed, and the few moments to regroup that Jack required.

He managed to uplink his laptop to the CIA database in order to complete a more thorough analysis of Surgit Gupta while Sydney cleaned up and changed. He had almost completely wiped from his mind the image of Sydney covered in blood, emerging from the stairs at the rear of the research center, and running full out toward the waiting van. Her speed told him she wasn't the one seriously injured. The time she'd spent in the building after signing off, however, were torturous minutes he would enjoy never reliving, and the crimson swashes that ran up to her elbows and spattered her face indicated that the extraction hadn't gone as planned. He hadn't bothered to ask when she climbed in, breathless, and told him to "Go!" Magrite wasn't joining them, and their operation had likely been blown.

She'd given him the broad strokes of the fight and Magrite's death. She'd spent considerably more time hypothesizing about the mysterious Katelyn that Magrite had died to protect. For his part, Jack agreed with her suspicion that Katelyn was probably Magrite's daughter, and had probably also been kidnapped. Neither knew what to make of Magrite's bizarre assertion that "She was the one." Finding Katelyn was another matter, and Jack couldn't shake the feeling that they weren't going to be able to do that until they had a better understanding of Gupta's motives. Beyond the fact that he was most likely the creator of the Marburg strain they were looking for, Jack was still unclear about Gupta's choice to kidnap Magrite rather than execute him. So Jack had set about the only course of action available to him until their next scheduled contact from APO, which was more than an hour away. He'd gone digging, and finally he'd found what he believed he was looking for.

Syd emerged from the bathroom, toweling off her wet hair. She'd put on a pair of black jeans and a white tank, and all evidence of the horrors she had just endured were mercifully gone except for a slight flush where she'd taken a punch. She was focused and calm, just what he needed her to be.

"Anything yet?" she asked, seating herself on the room's only bed and reaching for her black canvas sneakers.

"I think so," he replied, turning to face her.

"What?"

"Gupta has two sons. The eldest, Sayteesh, was admitted to the Kanpur Medical Center five days ago."

"What's wrong with him?" Sydney asked.

"I was able to hack into the hospital's database and pull up his chart. The initial symptoms were headache, fever, and an unusual rash."

Sydney didn't blink. "He's bringing his son into the family business, isn't he?"

"Looks like it to me. He didn't kidnap Magrite to prevent him from developing a cure that would make his weapon useless."

"He kidnapped him so he could cure his son," Sydney finished.

"The diagnosis of Marburg was confirmed twenty-four hours after Sayteesh was admitted. Magrite was taken from his hotel the next morning. I've also confirmed that Gupta has known Magrite for some time. There are guest lists from Proto-Chem events going back years that indicate that Magrite and Theodore Minden had been affiliated with Proto-Chem since they opened operations in India and Africa."

"But didn't you tell me that Gupta only recently joined Proto-Chem's board."

"They've all been at the same parties for years.

They knew each other. For all we know, Gupta got the idea to develop the Marburg strain from his interactions with Magrite."

"It also might explain how comfortable they were together when Gupta was questioning him," Sydney added. "You don't think Magrite had anything to do with the weapon, do you?" she asked.

"No," Jack replied. "Magrite has devoted the past ten years to eradicating viral hemorrhagic fevers. He didn't need Gupta's money. Omnifam has been funding him more than adequately. They added a research wing to the Regent's Clinic at Magrite's request almost two years ago, and he's been dividing his time between Johannesburg and Tshwane ever since. It looks like he was planning to make Tshwane his base of operations in the next few months, but he hadn't set up a permanent office there yet. Gupta, as a representative for Proto-Chem, also attended the Omnifam conference where Magrite delivered his early paper on gene therapy protocols. Gupta might have seen what no one else did, especially if he'd been working on the weaponized strain since the Angola outbreak in 2001."

"That Magrite was on the right track?"

"That's my guess. Then his son gets careless

with a delivery, contracts the virus, and Magrite is the first person Gupta thinks of."

"What about Katelyn?" Sydney asked.

"Insurance," he replied.

"The minute he finds out Magrite is dead, he's going to kill her."

"I know," Jack agreed.

"So where would he keep her?"

"No idea," Jack replied.

Sydney paused, thoughtful. "Does Gupta have any other freelancers on his payroll besides Aisi?"

"Not that we know of," Jack answered, picking up her train of thought.

"Where is Aisi now?"

Jack checked his watch. "I'll confirm it with operations, but if I'm right, he's on his way to Cairo. They'll change planes there before the next leg to Miami."

"We need someone on the ground in Cairo when he gets there," Sydney said.

"Agreed."

SOWETO, SOUTH AFRICA

Marshall was literally bouncing in and out of the range of the camera that was situated over the computer he was using for his teleconference with Vaughn and Dixon. Vaughn couldn't remember the last time he'd seen him so wound up.

Vaughn was seated next to Dixon, a laptop with a wireless satellite feed on the dashboard between them. They waited in the truck's passenger compartment for Marshall to pause for breath.

". . . contained the complete genetic code for each of the patients Magrite successfully treated," Marshall was saying.

Dixon had shared with Vaughn a little of his intel from Rhodes and Patterson just before the video conference call was patched through, but they hadn't had a chance to tell Marshall, who was rhapsodizing about the computer they'd found in Katelyn's room.

"The software . . . who the hell designed that database is all I want to know, but that's another conversation. Bottom line, I was right. The program was specifically created to analyze the genome and then code the vector that was created to inject into the patients. It's pure genius, guys, and I don't just toss that word around."

"So, it was fully automated," Vaughn interrupted.

"No!" Marshall almost shouted. "Didn't I mention that? I mean . . . wait . . . no, I didn't."

"Then it isn't really the missing piece we were looking for, is it?" Vaughn asked.

"It is and it isn't," Marshall replied.

Here we go again.

"The program is designed to allow the user to select and theoretically test gene therapy protocols. But it doesn't factor the permutations independently."

"What does that mean?" Dixon asked.

Marshall paused, apparently trying to make this piece of information as user friendly as possible.

"There are hundreds, maybe thousands, of variables that the program can't account for. It's math the program isn't designed to do. Basically the user can see the whole genetic code of the patient and then select the genes most likely to be affected positively by alterations. Those genes are then fed into the vector builder to create the DNA strand that will be inserted into the patient. It creates an exact blueprint. With that blueprint, creating the designer cure for each patient wouldn't have been nearly as time consuming as without. This is the only way Magrite could have used his protocol to cure as many people as he did in ten days. This is definitely how he did it."

"So Magrite performed the calculations that the program couldn't?" Vaughn interrupted. "I thought you said Einstein couldn't do that math in his head."

"Yeah, that's still a problem," Marshall agreed.

"It wasn't Magrite," Dixon said.

"What are you talking about?" Vaughn asked.

"Do you remember when I told you about Joshua Grey?" Dixon asked.

Vaughn was at a complete loss. "No." He shook his head.

"He's a pianist. He played at a benefit for autism a few years ago. Diane wanted to go, so I took her. He can't read or write, but when he wasn't calculating pi to a factor of over twenty-two thousand decimal places, he was playing classical pieces from memory that he'd only ever heard once."

"He was a savant?" Marshall interjected.

"You've never seen anything like it," Dixon added. "He had access to parts of his mind that normal people just don't have. It was extraordinary."

"Are you saying Magrite was a savant?" Marshall asked. "He couldn't have been. We wouldn't have missed that in our research. It's true that almost ten percent of all autistic people have heightened abilities, usually in the areas of math, art, music, and memory, but most of them also can't function in, you know, medical school."

Vaughn turned to Dixon, remembering what Angel and Grace had said about Katelyn's injury and subsequent abilities in math.

"Katelyn was?" he asked.

"The same Katelyn who had the entire collection of Barbie screen savers on her hard drive?" Marshall demanded.

"She suffered a traumatic head injury a few years ago. After that she started to demonstrate unique and unusual abilities, despite the fact that her other development processes lagged behind. She helped Cecilia Minden genetically engineer hybrids for her garden."

"And you think she was responsible for Magrite's success?" Vaughn asked, incredulous. "Is that possible?"

"Yes," Marshall replied before Dixon had a chance. "In fact, it's the only thing that makes sense, given what we know."

"She is eleven years old, guys," Vaughn insisted. "I don't care how brilliant she is; she doesn't become a genetic engineer at the age of eleven."

"She wouldn't have necessarily had to understand what she was doing," Marshall said. "Savants are highly capable in their specific areas of expertise—hence the term 'savant.' They tend to be able to remember volumes of information. Books they read—if they can read—cover to cover, forward and back. Many of them can calculate large numbers and see patterns. Their abilities can surpass the most complicated computers we've been able to design. A true savant, given precise parameters, could theoretically memorize an entire genome and automatically 'see' mathematical variances that could be corrected by an appropriate vector. She wouldn't know she was curing Marburg. She would just see the patterns and rearrange them so they were perfect. She would be compelled to rearrange them. It's what they do. They can't help it."

Vaughn sat with the incredible possibility for a moment before he said, "Didn't the neighbors say she is quite and shy . . . painfully shy? How do you figure out that a child like that even has those abilities?"

"It probably helps to be a molecular biologist," Dixon replied.

"You know, my mom always said I was pretty quiet as a child," Marshall added.

"The real question is, did her kidnappers know any of this?" Dixon continued. "Was she taken because they knew her role in Magrite's work, or just to keep him working?"

Before anyone could hazard a guess, Sloane's face appeared on the screen.

"Gentlemen, I hate to interrupt, but I've just heard from Jack and Sydney. Magrite is dead, but it seems likely that he was kidnapped to cure a case of Marburg in the family of his kidnapper, Surgit Gupta."

"We've just realized something pretty important, Mr. Sloane," Marshall interrupted.

"Katelyn Magrite, the good doctor's daughter, is a savant who is walking around with the ability to cure Marburg in her head?" Sloane asked.

"Um . . . yeah," Marshall replied, obviously disappointed that he'd been unable to drop this bombshell himself.

"I read you're preliminary analysis of the computer you found at the Minden home. That in conjunction with intel acquired from Jack lead me to the same conclusion," Sloane said simply.

"What did Jack say?" Vaughn demanded.

"Before he died, Magrite said that 'She was the

one.' By 'she' we assume he meant Katelyn. Magrite hadn't been able to cure Gupta's son. He wasn't stalling. He knew Gupta had Katelyn. If he'd been able to reproduce his results in Tshwane without her, he would have done it, if only to protect his daughter."

"So how are we going to find her?" Vaughn asked.

"You're going to Cairo immediately," Sloane replied. "There's a plane waiting for you in Johannesburg."

CAIRO, EGYPT

Aisi hadn't really slept since, well, he couldn't remember when. The last time he'd seen the sun he'd been dragging himself out of his hotel room bed, late for a lunch meeting with a potential new client who had suggested they meet again that evening at Raa. Then there had been the van, a helicopter, another van, and finally some sort of private plane with exceedingly comfortable seats. The alcohol and drug induced blackouts didn't count as rest, but had completely shot his internal clock. Truth be told, he had no idea how much time had passed since he'd last opened his eyes and his life had been his own. None of his captors had bothered to even hint at their final destination. If the strange woman from the bar and the bastard who had interrogated him were any indication, he presumed he was heading for America.

Good luck to them.

He had more than a hundred thousand American dollars at his disposal. He didn't know what kind of legal defense that would buy him in the states, but in Kanpur it would have retained the services of a top attorney for many months. The interrogation had been illegal. He hadn't been advised of his rights. He hadn't been offered counsel. The partial confession he'd given them would never be admissible.

The thoughts that had kept him awake all these hours, however, were the rumors that had been circulating for years about the American government's ability to bypass these legal interrogation procedures when dealing with suspected or known terrorists. Aisi had known captured men to disappear down black holes, never to be heard from again. It was far too likely for his comfort that he was headed for one of those holes himself, and all the money in the world wouldn't get him out of it.

He had felt the subtle shift in his stomach that

indicated the plane was headed down. He was momentarily jarred but not really stunned when the plane's landing gear hit a runway and taxied quickly to a stop.

Refueling, he imagined.

Suddenly he was pulled from his seat and forced down a short aisle before being all but thrown down a short stairway.

The first sensation he was aware of was an oppressive heat, which should have been accompanied by a blinding light, even through the dark sack that had been placed over his face.

When the bag was removed, he found himself surrounded by six armed men, all wearing black. They were on an otherwise deserted airstrip. There was probably an airport nearby, but in the darkness he found it difficult to get any sense of direction.

"Here they are," he heard one of the men behind him say.

Glancing to his right, Aisi saw that a black sedan had just parked a hundred meters from their position at the end of a dirt road. Two men climbed out. Only when they got closer did he realize that one of them, the taller of the two, was black. The other, more slight of frame, was white.

They approached Aisi quickly and came to a

stop less than a meter in front of him. The white one spoke first.

"You left Magrite in Kanpur on Monday night. But that wasn't the end of your mission, was it?" he asked.

For the moment Aisi chose to maintain a defiant silence.

"From there you caught a flight to Johannesburg. You were sent to Soweto, where you kidnapped an eleven-year-old girl. You killed a British citizen in the process, but that doesn't concern me now. Where did you take the little girl?"

Admitting to kidnapping had been one thing. Admitting to murder would be quite another, and despite the small man's assurances that he was only interested in the girl, Aisi was certain such an admission would come back to haunt him later.

"I don't know what you're talking about," he replied.

"Yes, you do," the white man insisted, stepping closer.

Aisi wasn't alarmed. This man, whoever he was, did not fill him with the same sense of fear he'd felt in the presence of his first interrogator.

"Go to hell," he said, confident that as long as

he chose to, he could control this situation.

Then the white man smiled faintly and shook his head. He tossed a glance at his companion, who stood silently beside him. Maybe the other man was the "bad cop" in this little game. Problem was, he didn't frighten Aisi either.

"I'm going to give you one last chance to tell me what I want to know," the "good cop" said.

"And then what?" Aisi replied. "You should have sent the other man, the one who was there when I was first captured. That man had death in his eyes. His were the eyes of a man who would not hesitate to kill to get what he wanted. You are not that man. There is pain in your eyes . . . despair . . . fear . . . but not death."

The white man did not blink. He raised his chin slightly and nodded briefly to the armed guards behind him. Aisi watched without concern as the guards filed back onto the plane, leaving him alone with the other two. They didn't speak. The black man moved to stand behind Aisi and, clutching the top of Aisi's shoulders, forced him to kneel before his partner.

Still Aisi's resolve did not waver.

Then the white man removed a 9mm handgun

from the holster that had been hidden under his jacket, and after releasing the safety he pressed it squarely to Aisi's forehead, just above the bridge of his nose.

"Really?" the white man finally said.

Aisi searched his mind for a glib response. His mouth was suddenly parched, and nothing would come out.

The white man met his gaze, and for the first time since his arrival Aisi considered the possibility that he might have judged this man a little too quickly.

"Tell me more about my eyes," he said softly.

CHAPTER 8

KANPUR, INDIA

The word "house" did not come to mind when considering Surgit Gupta's living quarters and the surrounding environs in Kanpur. Less still, the word "home." "Compound" seemed a more appropriate title for the more than nine-thousand-square-foot mansion situated behind cement walls, walls that had been covered with whitewashed stucco to make their eighteen feet of height appear more stately than imposing.

"Everything about the place says 'Keep Out,'" Sydney mused as she and her father hastily scanned the computer-generated layout they had just received. They had parked two hundred meters from the estate's rear entrance in their mobile operations center, the black van they'd had since the start of the mission.

"It was certainly designed with an eye toward security," her father agreed.

"Those towers at each corner," Sydney pointed out.

"If it were my home and I were a black-market weapons dealer, I'd post shooters there," Jack replied.

It was a little past one in the afternoon, local time. The villa was something of an oddity, set in the hills that swept up to the north of the city. There were six other homes, spaced well apart along the recently paved stretch of road that led to the black iron gates at the front. For the surveillance part of their mission, Jack and Sydney had chosen a dirt path surrounded by trees to the west of the structure. The path narrowed over the next quarter mile as it climbed to the peak of the hill where it dead-ended.

"I'm going to check the infrared," Sydney said, grabbing the specialized binoculars from her pack and moving toward the van's rear windows. The windows had been tinted black, of course, but did not affect the infrared capabilities of the device.

Jack had intentionally positioned the van to give them the best unobstructed view of the compound from the most discreet distance. The binoculars were equipped with high-powered zoom capabilities that easily allowed Sydney to focus her search on only the area of interest. She first swept the grounds outside the gated wall. She discovered three armed figures walking a lazy perimeter. She observed their paths for a full six minutes and found the timing lapse that would leave either the front or rear drive untended for a minimum of thirty seconds and a maximum of almost two minutes.

She then focused her attention on the house and its outbuildings. The large building that occupied the center of the complex had three stories. Essentially a large rectangle with four turrets, one on each corner, it was accessible by six doors and dozens of windows on the main level. Four figures were seated in what was most likely the kitchen.

Lunchtime, Sydney mused.

Each of the towers was occupied by a solitary individual, as Jack had suggested, but only one of the four was standing alert at his post. The other three sat in place, either reading or talking on cell phones.

Two figures walked calmly through the house in an unhurried gait that Sydney always associated with patrolling. Only one of the upstairs rooms was occupied. A small figure, clearly not an adult, sat before what was most likely a television set. The posture and positioning of the hands gave the impression that someone was playing a video game.

Possibly Katelyn.

Sydney was about to continue her search, just to make sure she hadn't missed anyone, when her attention was pulled back to the small figure. Every few seconds the outline of the figure blurred slightly along what would have been the person's back, making them briefly larger, almost humpbacked, before returning to normal. The distortion was so slight as to make it almost imperceptible, or at the very least easy to write off as interference or a signal degradation due to her distance from the targets. It took almost a minute of constant observation for her to realize what she was seeing.

Someone roughly the same size as the figure

she could clearly identify was seated, in relation to Sydney, directly behind the individual she had already distinguished. That person's body heat was being picked up as part of the first person rather than scanning clearly as a second individual. Only their motion, what appeared now to be a slight rocking back and forth, was visible.

Katelyn, Sydney suddenly knew.

"We've got three guards on the perimeter and ten adults in the house," she advised Jack, returning to the schematic and pointing out their locations. "The towers are manned, but no one seems to be on any kind of high alert. There are two others moving regularly throughout the first and second floors. The four in the kitchen could be hostiles, or could be family members. There are at least two children upstairs, here." She pointed to the room.

"Which might mean they haven't been alerted to Magrite's death yet," Jack suggested.

"It's possible," Sydney agreed. "Either that or they're confident in their abilities to defend this position."

"It's a minimum of nine against two at this point," Jack observed, "with an additional four to six noncombatants."

"I don't like those numbers," Sydney replied. "Not so much the nine. It's the family and especially the children I'm worried about."

"So we need to take advantage of the fact that they're not being quite as cautious as they ought, and disable as many of the pros as we can before we get in there," Jack decided.

"Works for me," Sydney replied.

Ten minutes later Jack had hacked into the wireless communications line that was being used by the contingent of armed guards, and satisfied himself by monitoring their chatter that none of them was aware that Magrite had been compromised.

He listened with more pride than concern as Sydney disabled all three of the perimeter guards, using the time-honored sneak attack. As soon as each man went down, Jack sent a surge along their individual channels to disable their communication signals. If they were contacted by any of the others, the line would send only a sharp burst of static, which would appear at first to be a malfunction or an indication that the man in question had wandered briefly out of range.

Six to go.

Once all three had been rendered unconscious, he gave Sydney a few moments to alter her appearance as needed, then watched from the van as she began to stumble up the main road toward the gates in cutoff jean shorts and her white tank. Her hair hung loosely about her face, and she walked on one sling-backed red high heel, holding the other shoe in her hand. It was a fair imitation of a damsel in distress. Given the damsel in question, Jack didn't doubt that she would quickly attract the attention of at least two or three of the other guards.

She reached the front gates and, shielding her eyes from the glaring sun with one hand, peered through the iron bars. The comm channel was instantly activated as tower one and two called out almost simultaneously, "Unknown female approaching north gate."

"I'm on it," a deep voice replied.

A few moments later Jack watched as Sydney's face broke into a wide smile and she waved sweetly at the man approaching the gate. The moment he reached her, she put on her best West Virginia accent and began a long rambling statement that included the salient points. She was lost, her car was damaged, over a mile away, she needed help.

The man immediately did the most he should have done in the situation. He chastised her for trespassing on private property, to instill an appropriate level of unease in the unwelcome stranger, then he more politely offered to allow her to use his cell phone.

"Oh . . . I don't have anyone to call," Sydney replied sadly.

The guard sized her up. Had Sydney not been Jack's daughter, this would have been more amusing to watch. There had been many times in the past four years when Sydney's work as an undercover operative had come into harsh and painful conflict with his quite natural desire to protect his daughter. Though circumstances had forced him to prepare his daughter at an extremely early age for potentially dire circumstances, he had always secretly hoped that the programming that "Project Christmas" had instilled in her had not been the decisive factor in her choice to become an agent. He would have much preferred to see her bored out of her mind as some sort of professional, or perhaps pursuing her on-again, off-again romance with teaching. It would have been too much to hope that she would have been outrageously happy and fulfilled in her work and personal relationships. But he would never forget the strange knot of pain, anger, and fear that had accompanied the revelation that she had been recruited by and joined SD-6. It was not what he had ever wanted. But there was some comfort in the knowledge that as long as she was working as an agent, he could be there to watch over her.

Working side by side on operations such as this, he still found it impossible to watch her work with the same detached professionalism he would have had with any other partner or team. He had to admit, however, that she was spectacular at her job, and this instance was no exception.

After a few unconvincing attempts to dissuade her, the guard eventually opened the gate and called for assistance. And within minutes Sydney could be seen flirting her way back down the road away from the van, accompanied by two of Gupta's men toward her nonexistent broken-down vehicle.

The moment they're out of visual range of the complex, they won't know what hit them.

He didn't have to wait long for the call.

"Phoenix to Raptor."

"Go ahead," he replied.

"You're clear to enter. Five are down. I'll meet you at the front door."

Jack immediately started the van and pulled onto the paved road. As he came within a few meters of the gate, he caught sight of Sydney running full speed toward him. He didn't bother to stop. The guard Sydney had first enthralled had been too interested in her obvious charms to remember to latch the gate. Jack nudged the van between them, forcing them open. But he left the van parked between the posts on which the two iron doors were hinged, to avoid being trapped within the complex if what was about to come proved to be more difficult than he had anticipated.

Within moments one of the remaining four guards was at the front door, half-running toward the van, waving at him to stop and turn back.

Jack didn't hesitate. Leaping from the driver's seat, he already had his 9mm in his hand, and the man was down before he got within ten meters of the van.

Sydney had managed to trade her pumps for sneakers she'd left along one of the walls when she'd disabled the sentries. Jack tossed her gun to her as she threw herself on the ground behind the van. Two more men had just emerged from the front of the house, making no pretense about their intentions, their semiautomatic rifles trained on the van.

Jack quickly dispatched the first, aiming a perfect shot to the center of his forehead. Sydney obviously had the second in her sights. He was down only seconds after his companion.

By Jack's count that left at least one more guard. He paused, still covered by the door of the van, listening for the inevitable.

Then it came, the series of shots from above, raining down on the pavement and the van's hood.

He couldn't get a clear and immediate sense of the direction, but Sydney was apparently way ahead of him. Another two shots rang out, and a man fell from the top of the northeast tower to the ground-level rock bed that landscaped the perimeter of the house like a moat.

Sydney joined her father behind the driver's side door. Shouts and cries of alarm came from deep inside the house. The front door remained open, not the least bit inviting.

Their eyes met. Jack nodded slightly, and

Sydney ran for the front door. He took a moment to cover her, but as no more fire erupted from any direction, he was soon at her heels trailing her into the house.

They made their way into the wide entry hall, a ghastly concoction of stained wood, crystal, and mirrors, and each began to methodically clear their separate sides of the house. Jack reached the kitchen, where he found three terrified women huddled around a squat round woman in her late seventies; they clustered behind a granite bar that divided the cooking and dining areas.

"Raptor, the house is clear," Jack heard Syd through his earpiece. "I'm going after Katelyn."

"Copy that," he replied as he raised his weapon and trained it on the unfortunate group of women.

"Good afternoon, Mrs. Gupta," he said, addressing the eldest and calmest of the four. "I believe your son brought you a guest a few days ago."

One of the women shrieked at his words and was silenced with a slap from Surgit's mother.

"We did not harm anyone," she said defiantly.

"I'm glad to hear it," he replied. "I'm sorry for the trouble, but we'll be on our way in a few minutes."

Two of the women sobbed softly. Mrs. Gupta made no move to comfort them. She stood absolutely still, both angry and proud, and seemed to be calculating the odds that she might find any way to gain the upper hand in this little confrontation.

"Now, now," Jack warned.

Jack had often wondered what precisely turned one human being into a monster while so many others lived their lives doing little or no real damage to the rest of the world around them. Staring into the steel gray eyes of Surgit Gupta's mother, he thought he saw at least part of an answer, at least in this case.

We are what we are made to be.

In this case perhaps nature, but definitely nurture had been stacked against Gupta.

"May I at least have the pleasure of knowing who it is that has entered my home without my permission?" Mrs. Gupta asked coldly.

Jack considered the available responses. Despite her diminutive stature, Mrs. Gupta stood before him still proud and arrogant.

What a piece of work.

"Can you keep a secret, Mrs. Gupta?" Jack asked calmly.

The woman nodded; a flicker of a smile passing ever so briefly across her lips.

"So can I," Jack said.

Nine thousand six hundred seventy-one.

Nine thousand six hundred seventy-two.

Nine thousand . . .

Aunt Cecilia had gone away.

. . . six hundred . . .

Daddy hadn't come for her.

. . . seventy-three . . .

She didn't know who the red and purple boy was who seemed to love nothing more than the loud pounding that pumped its way out of his earphones and the bright images shooting and dying on the television screen. She knew that he smelled funny.

That tickles.

He didn't seem to mind that she sat so close to him.

. . . Nine thousand . . six hundred . . .

He didn't have a choice. If he protested again, his gamma, the old woman who was also red but sometimes a clap of thunder, would return and scream at him and he would be afraid.

. . . seventy-four, seventy-five, seventy-six, seventy-seven . . .

Why did all of those people on the television have to die like that?

The counting made it better. Sometime, pretty soon, the game would be over and there would be other things to count, other bright colors to discover . . . maybe sounds that were more like bees singing or kitties dancing. Pink sounds. Pink sounds were her favorite.

. . . Nine thousand . . .

When is Daddy coming? They promised her that Daddy would be here soon.

Daddy was green and smelled like the ocean. Not that she had ever been to the ocean. She had seen it, from far above. Daddy had told her all about the ocean. And when he told her about it, she knew how it smelled. It was a pink smell.

Oh, Daddy . . please . . six hundred seventy-eight . . .

"Katelyn?"

She didn't know that voice.

The boy didn't seem to know or care about it either. He just kept shooting the people on the television.

"Katelyn . . . can you hear me?"

Suddenly the boy stopped shooting.

"Hey . . . who are—"

But he didn't have a chance to finish his question.

There were arms attached to the voice. Arms that smelled like rain and leaves changing, and then she was being lifted up and up.

"Don't be afraid, Katelyn. We're going to get you out of here."

She didn't open her eyes. She was afraid if she did that the arms would go away. She didn't know the arms, but she liked that they smelled like wind rushing over a bluebird's wing.

Maybe the arms would take her to Daddy.

All she knew for sure was that between the rain and the leaves and the rushing wind, there was nothing more to count right now and that felt better.

It felt almost pink.

Twenty miles away, in a private wing of the Kanpur Medical Center's intensive care unit, Surgit Gupta stood a lonely vigil behind a partition of glass that separated him from Sayteesh.

Sayteesh was dying.

And it's my fault.

It was ridiculous to keep evaluating and reexamining the choices that had brought him to this moment. His eldest son had always wanted to enter his father's business, and that had never seemed to be a difficult choice. True, Surgit had worked the hours and made the compromises he had over the years so that Sayteesh, Aman, and Vivek would have been spared the need to work at all, let alone in the family business. But Sayteesh had been so passionate in his plea and so steadfast in his determination to make something of himself—*like his father*—that Surgit hadn't had the heart to say no the twentieth time Sayteesh had asked.

The training Sayteesh had received had been even more rigorous than most of Surgit's other employees. But Sayteesh had been a good student. His faith in the work to be done had been both pure and reassuring.

There were dark nights over the years when voices of doubt had taunted Surgit, questioning his commitment to the course. But always he had silenced them. There had been nothing—nothing—in the world he would not do to make sure that he and his family were as protected as it was possible to be in this world.

He did not concern himself with right and wrong. Who was to say that anything could be so labeled in the world today? All that was right was that which was profitable. The rest would take care of itself. So many suffered. So many needed their misery to end. Perhaps someday there would be a world where such decisions did not have to be made, but today was not that day. Today you had what you could acquire . . . nothing else.

Except that there were things you lost along the way.

He could barely make out the rise and fall of breath still wavering, however shallow, in his son's chest. Sayteesh's arms were wrapped in gauze to ease the painful and horrendous itching that had come with the bright red bumps that now covered his chest and back as well. His fingers were tinted a permanent shade of red. Was it fever, or the blood that had come and would come again as his body lost forever its ability to stem the tide?

None of this was as frightening as his son's face, visible in the faint flickering light only as a pallid reminder that Surgit had chosen poorly. The worst of the fever seemed to have passed, but Sayteesh's face—his eyes—stared at a place Surgit could not see. Was it filled with horrors, or peace? There was such final resignation in Sayteesh's face. It was made all the more terrifying because Surgit had no idea how to reach his son in that far away country of his nightmares.

No.

He would not allow himself to think that way. There was still hope. Arthur would not let him down. Arthur had been naïve for most of his brilliant life. But, like Surgit, Arthur had the ability to separate motive from action. A boy who did not deserve to die was dying for his father's mistakes. Arthur could save him. This was a simple equation. Evaluation of right and wrong might come later. For now there was only the problem to be solved, and Arthur would solve it.

Then, perhaps, they could be friends again.

Well, they had never been friends. But Surgit had always had the utmost respect for Arthur's work, even when the others had called him too optimistic.

Arthur need never know the truth. It would be far better that, once this disastrous situation had been made right, they never discuss that it was over dinner several years ago that Arthur had first helped Surgit see the potential in all viral hemorrhagic fevers, but particularly Marburg. Had Arthur left London early that night, rather than accept Surgit's last-minute invitation, perhaps none of them would be where they were right now.

But it didn't matter.

Here they were. Arthur would do his job. Sayteesh would be cured. And the rest was a problem for tomorrow.

He was roused from these troubling thoughts by the sharp beep of his cellular phone. Through the crackle of static—Why was it so hard to get a decent signal in this wretched place?—he could barely make out the voice of Sunil, his personal driver.

Sunil had accompanied him on his last visit to Arthur, just to check the biologist's progress. He had then dropped Surgit at the hospital and been dismissed to run a few errands. Surgit would not leave the hospital again until his son was either cured or dead.

His heart leaped as he thought he heard Sunil say the word "Magrite."

Arthur had succeeded. He knew it. Now if there was just still time . . .

". . . dead . . ."

Surgit paused, then moved away from the window through which he'd been watching his son, hoping to find a clearer signal.

". . . Did you hear what I said?" Sunil was saying.

"No, pl-please repeat," Surgit stammered. "Has something happened to Dr. Magrite?"

"Dr. Magrite is dead, sir."

It was unthinkable. It was unacceptable. *How had this happened?*

"When? How?" Surgit struggled to find the most important questions.

"The research center was infiltrated, sir. We're still searching through what's left of the lab. Sunny and Chand were killed. Hrithik is on his way to the hospital now. I don't know if he'll make it either, sir."

This was ridiculous. Magrite was a minor scientist pursuing fringe theories. No one would have expended the resources necessary to mount such an assault in only three days. Surgit had counted on this when he had chosen to pursue this course. True, the attack on Tshwane would have caught the attention of the worldwide intelligence community, but only *three days later*? Perhaps he had underestimated the fervor with which the Americans and Europeans were working to stamp out global terrorism. Given all they had on their respective plates, he had counted on remaining a low priority until the sale of the new strain was complete. Still . . . *three days later*?

"Sir?" Sunil's sharp tone refocused his thoughts.

"What is it?"

"We have found several items that were left in a crawl space above the lab. Audio and video monitoring devices . . quite advanced. It was definitely the Americans."

Well, that was interesting.

"We've reviewed the recordings. A lone white female was on-site. She tried to extract Magrite, but he was reluctant to go with her initially. She must have had help on the outside. There are coded communications between her and someone she called 'Raptor.' Magrite's last words were . . . well, sir . . . they don't make any sense."

"Let me hear them, from the original source," Surgit demanded.

A low background hum and Sunil's frustrated bark of orders accompanied the few tense moments that elapsed before Surgit heard the distinct sounds of gunfire and shouting that had preceded Magrite's last minutes of life. He listened as the rescuer—definitely American—moved to Magrite and finally understood that the garbled sound he was trying to make was his daughter's name. "They don't know . . . she was the one . . . not me . . ."

Gupta's heart stopped in his chest. Suddenly it all made sense. Arthur hadn't been stalling. He'd had help developing his miraculous cure. But that help could not have come in the form of an eleven-year-old girl.

That's impossible.

Unless . . .

His mind raced as he struggled to go back to that dinner, a little over two years ago in London. They had talked of so many things. Arthur's work had taken center stage, of course. But he'd spent most of the dessert course talking about a patient he'd refused to name . . . a young girl who had suffered a traumatic head injury and who had since begun to display remarkable and heretofore unseen facilities in math and art. He'd only accepted the invitation to that particular Proto-Chem conference because he'd intended to meet with a neurologist who specialized in autism.

Surgit shook his head sadly. He'd had the key to Sayteesh's cure in his hands all the time. And he hadn't known.

A wave of nauseating fear coursed through him. Those who had come for Magrite had not known of Katelyn's existence until Magrite's last words. He had only discovered the girl when researching the viability of simply paying Magrite to cure Sayteesh, when he had seen the unusual transfers to Soweto. He replayed the conversation in his head until he was able to put his finger on the source of the fear that now wracked him.

The American woman was going after Katelyn. Katelyn was the only person who might still be able to cure his son. But more terrifying was the possibility that she would discover Katelyn's whereabouts while she was still being looked after by—

"Get my mother on the phone at once!" Gupta barked. "She must be warned."

"I've already done so, sir." Sunil replied.

Of course he had. There was a reason Surgit

paid his driver a salary most of Surgit's associates thought insanely high.

"I'm almost there now."

"Is she all right?" Surgit demanded.

"There is no answer, sir. She didn't pick up the house phone, or her private cell."

Surgit refused to allow this sudden turn of events to drown him in the rushing torrents of panic.

"Call me the moment you arrive," he said as calmly as he could. "I want Katelyn Magrite brought to this hospital as soon as you've confirmed my mother's safety."

"Yes, sir."

Surgit resisted the urge to smash his cell phone into the floor for being the method of transmission of such horrible news. Instead he returned to the window and watched as the nurse who had entered while he was otherwise occupied now checked his son's vital signs and replaced the damp cloth on his forehead with a new, cool one. He forced himself not to look away as she completed her check by cleaning a trickle of blood that had run down his son's left cheek from his eyes.

This was still a good sign. Death would not be

assured until Sayteesh's fever broke completely and his internal organs began to shut down. The doctors believed that was only hours away, but if Katelyn could be made to see reason . . . to help them as she had helped her father. It was irrelevant. She would be forced to help. Even a child understood that it was better to be alive than dead.

The cell phone beeped again. Surgit moved to the best reception site in the room and answered. He listened with cool detachment to Sunil's report of what he had found at his mother's home. It was not shock that sustained him. It was rage.

Once he understood that the plans he had made so carefully and paid so extravagantly for had come to naught, he briefly considered the range of retaliatory options open to him. Then he realized revenge could wait.

Sayteesh could still be saved.

"Find the little girl," he snarled into the phone before slamming it shut and throwing it to the floor with such force that it broke into several useless pieces.

CHAPTER 9

NEPAL

Four hours after leaving the Gupta compound and beginning their long journey north, Katelyn smiled for the first time since Sydney had laid eyes on her. Finding that smile had been as challenging a search as any Sydney had ever undertaken.

Katelyn had spent the first several hours of the trip curled in as tiny a ball as she could manage, below the bench in the back of the van.

Sydney had tried in vain to get her to sit in the van's only rear seat, strapped safely in with the seat belt. But Katelyn would have none of it. Given all she'd been through in the last several days, Syd had thought it best she not traumatize the child further by physically forcing her to do anything she didn't want to. The chains that had held Aisi had been stowed. Knowing that if they succeeded in rescuing the little girl the van should be as hospitable as possible, Sydney had done what she could to make everything around her appear unthreatening . . . a difficult task under the circumstances. Jack had refused to even stop for fuel and regroup until they were more than three hundred kilometers from Kanpur, heading north-northeast toward Nepal.

Their final destination, a CIA safe house in Lhasa, Tibet, was only another five hundred kilometers away. But given the roads between Gorakhpur, where they'd stopped to purchase food and blankets, and Lhasa, it would most likely be a journey of six or seven more hours.

Katelyn had fallen into an uneasy sleep. Sydney made her way carefully to the back of the van. The often treacherous mountain road they were traversing meant that bumps and jolts were both frequent and unavoidable. With a firm hand on the low bench that ran along the van's side wall, Sydney seated herself Indian-style beside the makeshift pallet she had created for Katelyn, and gently pulled the edges of the quilt flecked with gold and yellow stars over the little girl's shoulders. Sydney took a moment to study the sweet face in repose. Her coarse black hair was pinned into unruly braids atop her head. Countless wisps sought to free themselves from the confines of the pattern creating a halo of short curls. In contrast, fine and very delicate light brown hairs formed a graceful arch above each eye. They blended almost imperceptibly into her pale mocha skin. Patches of freckles burst forth like fields of pale daisies on her cheeks, flowing freely across her small stub of a nose. Her lips were her most arresting feature. Full and fair, they formed almost a perfect bow shape above a firm chin. There was no tension in them as she blew soft brushes of air with each breath of sleep.

Her eyes opened quickly, as if she'd been startled awake. Deep blue with splinters of gold, her eyes were instantly tense with trepidation, and her little mouth became a tight line.

"It's okay," Sydney said as soothingly as possible.

Katelyn seemed to consider whether or not this

was really the case. Her eyes studied Sydney's face as if she could learn more of the truth by what she saw than by what she heard.

"You're going to be fine now," Sydney continued. "No one is going to hurt you."

Katelyn's eyes dropped to the blanket Sydney had tucked around her. She tried to sit up, and Sydney moved a gentle hand to her back to help her steady herself. Katelyn's eyes did not return to Sydney's face for a long moment. They remained fixed on the blanket, then moved slowly up the arms of the heavy black coat Sydney wore to keep out the worst of the cold. The van was great for APO's purposes, but it wasn't designed to be the most comfortable passenger vehicle. What little warmth the heater blew out barely made it past the front seats.

Sydney saw Katelyn shudder, and then worriedly asked, "Are you warm enough? Would you like to wear this coat?"

Katelyn didn't respond. Instead she cast her eyes down to the blanket, where they remained glued.

"I don't know about you," Sydney said, trying another tack, "but I'm pretty hungry." She moved to a cardboard box Jack had stocked at their last stop with crackers, dried meat, fruits, and nuts, and rummaged in it until she'd found a fair assortment. Moments later she returned with a little of everything—including a canteen of fresh water—and did her best to spread them enticingly out before the girl; anything to tempt her from her solitude.

Katelyn didn't take an immediate interest in the food, but Sydney was not easily discouraged. She couldn't know if or how well her previous captors had fed her, but it had been hours since anyone's last meal, and she had to be at least a little hungry. The little girl's eyes turned briefly to look at the food set before her, but immediately returned to their point of focus on the blanket. Her lips started to move silently. Sydney couldn't make out what she was saying at first, but after a moment Sydney realized that Katelyn was counting something . . . she knew not what. Taking the bull by the horns, Sydney made much of grabbing a piece of dried fruit and biting down on it noisily.

"Mmmm," Sydney said, munching on a dried apple and washing it down with a swig of water. "I love apples," she said kindly.

Katelyn did not meet her gaze, but said softly, "Green."

Sydney paused, wondering if this was a question

or a comment. The apples had been skinned before they were dried, and little of their natural sweetness remained, but if it would capture Katelyn's interest . . . At least she was no longer actively counting.

"They might have been green. I don't know. I'm not sure what kind of apples grow nearby. They're awfully good, though," she finished, taking another bite.

"They're a green fruit," Katelyn said almost stubbornly.

"Where I'm from, my favorite green apples are called Granny Smith apples," Sydney replied.

Katelyn fixed her with a fierce gaze. It was almost as if they had been playing a game and Katelyn had suddenly discovered that Sydney was cheating.

"Green . . . like a unicorn's horn," Katelyn said firmly, as if everyone should know this.

Sydney paused, at a loss. She'd been fully briefed by Vaughn as to what little APO knew of the child's mental state. She'd taken a cursory glance at the analysis of autistic savants APO's research department had hurriedly put together and transmitted to them in the first few hours of their journey. She was prepared for Katelyn to be anything from completely nonverbal or non-responsive to highly strung and prone to tantrums. Looking at her and sensing her absolute certainty, however, Sydney realized that Katelyn's psychology and physiology were decidedly not "normal" for either autistic children or the savants she'd read about. If Sydney hadn't known her history, or hadn't believed along with everyone else that Katelyn was the key to her father's miraculous work, she would have been hard pressed to see anything but a normal—albeit shy—and incredibly imaginative child.

She decided to take a chance. There had been one interesting paragraph in her notes that had referenced an extremely high-functioning adult savant who had been able to talk at great length about his perceptions of the world around him. The numbers, even the mind-numbingly huge ones he could calculate in a split second, weren't actually numbers at all in his head. They were sounds. "Two" was the sound of hands clapping. "Zero" was an ocean wave washing over a beach.

Biting into another piece of fruit, possibly a dried pear, Sydney said, "Brown . . . like a bird digging for a worm."

Katelyn's eyes snapped up and gazed fervently into hers. Sydney grabbed another pear and offered it to her.

Katelyn considered for a moment, then grabbed it quickly and brought it to her nose. After a few quick sniffs, she put it in her mouth and chewed quickly.

"No, no, no," she said, shaking her head. "Pears are not brown . . . they're violet."

Her eyes met Sydney's again, almost expectantly. Sydney took another bite and seemed to consider Katelyn's assessment.

"I still say brown," she replied playfully.

The corners of Katelyn's mouth curled faintly up. Her eyes became appraising, as if she knew she was being teased. She turned her attention to the array of foodstuffs Sydney had spread before her, and finally settling on a light cracker, she shoved it into her mouth and chewed noisily. Then she offered Sydney a piece. Sydney took it and began to chew with equal zeal.

"Brown," Katelyn said solemnly.

Sydney chewed a little more, then swallowed.

"Brown," she agreed.

Then . . . Katelyn smiled.

Maybe it was true of all children . . . that when they smiled openly and without reserve, it was almost impossible not to feel a deep and simple warmth creep up from the center of your chest until your face formed a smile of its own. Sydney hadn't spent that much time around infants or youngsters in the past few years, and this simple connection she had forged was a visceral reminder that someday she was going to have to choose whether or not motherhood was anywhere in her life's plan. She felt herself smiling back, and an intense desire to be positively goofy surged through her.

She grabbed a handful of nuts and offered them to Katelyn. Taking some of her own, they chewed for a moment in pleasant silence, until Katelyn blurted out, "Orange!" Sydney agreed and was rewarded with another smile . . . then a giggle.

They made their way through the entire meal in this way, Katelyn growing more open and articulate every moment.

Finally, when they were both more than sated, Katelyn pulled her blanket around her more tightly and asked, "Why is it so cold?"

"I'm sorry," Sydney replied. "But I promise, tomorrow we'll be somewhere warm again."

"Is my daddy there?" Katelyn asked.

Sydney paused. She didn't want to lie to the little girl, but she also didn't think this was the moment to explain to her that her life had changed forever. Not without also being able to offer her the faintest sense of what the future held for her.

"No," she replied, then asked, "Do you miss him very much?"

Katelyn considered the question seriously.

"Sometimes," she said softly, "but not all the time. Mostly he wants to talk about the other children and their colors."

"Their colors?" Sydney couldn't help but ask.

Katelyn nodded. "It's fun," she added, "but not fun like with Aunt Ceci."

"Can you tell me about the other children?" Sydney asked, worried that she was pushing it.

Katelyn shrugged simply. "The first time I see them, they don't make sense. Their colors are mixed up and their numbers don't work. Sowalzi, he was the last one my daddy showed me, he was all purple and black, but he wanted to be blue."

"And you . . . you could . . . help him be blue?" Sydney asked.

"Of course," Katelyn said, and nodded. "Blue like the sky at night. It was better that way. Happier. It made more sense. Just like the numbers for Aunt Ceci's roses. They want to be one thing, but when you put them together, sometimes they can be something even more beautiful."

Sydney took a deep breath as the full force of Katelyn's abilities rained down on her. For reasons no one could yet explain, this sweet little girl's mind was able to see beyond numbers and complicated calculations straight through to the "truth" of a person's genetic makeup. Sydney didn't know what the color references meant. They were the factors of the equation in Katelyn's mind—a mind that would probably never be understood in its true glory, only in its usefulness.

How that ability translated to the colors she assigned to other objects, the food, for example, was also a mystery. But a mystery that Sydney wouldn't have minded spending a great deal more time exploring.

She found herself reaching out to gently caress Katelyn's cheek. Before she knew it, the little girl had swooped into her arms, holding her in a hug that made it difficult to breathe.

"You're such a good girl," Sydney whispered softly.

At this, Katelyn pulled away and, gazing solemnly up at her, said, "So are you."

Sydney smiled as brightly as she could through the tears forming in her eyes.

"You are silver and gold," Katelyn said. "But don't worry. One day you will be as bright as the sun."

"Are silver and gold happy colors?" Sydney asked.

Katelyn shook her head sadly. "They are some of the strongest, but not usually the happiest."

"Do people ever change colors?" Sydney asked, a strange electric shyness overwhelming her. "Do silver and gold always become bright?"

Katelyn looked directly into Sydney's eyes. She remained quiet for a moment, and Sydney thought she saw Katelyn's lips moving again . . . counting.

"No, I'm right," Katelyn said after almost a minute had passed. "Everyone can change. Your silver and gold want to be starlight. You can be that too, if you let yourself. It's in your eyes."

Sydney couldn't know if Katelyn was speaking from some deep pool of knowledge that most people would never connect with, or from the fancy of her imagination. She couldn't imagine how it was possible, but something in the girl's firm set of jaw and studious expression suggested the former.

"What's the happiest color?" Sydney asked.

"Aunt Ceci," Katelyn replied. "The palest pink."

After a moment she added, "I wish everyone wanted to be pink."

"Me too," Sydney replied. She didn't know what "pink" meant to Katelyn. But Cecilia had been, for all intents and purposes, Katelyn's mother. If all of Sydney's hopes and dreams about her own mother could have been wrapped in a package before she'd ever learned the truth, if the sadness and simple love she had felt every time she'd looked at pictures of her mother from her childhood could have been wrapped up in one color . . . well, pink was as close as any.

LHASA, TIBET

They reached the safe house, high in the hills north of Lhasa, a few hours later without incident. Sydney had fallen asleep nestled beside Katelyn less than an hour earlier. Jack had heard their whispers and giggles over the roar of the engine that bounced around the van, but had been unable to make out most of their conversation, though he knew near the end there had been spirited discussion about the color pink in all of its permutations. After that there had been silence, and when he peered over his seat and saw the two sleeping figures nesting so comfortably, he hesitated to wake them.

But the sight of soft brushes of white breath coming from their partially opened mouths reminded him that, charming as this might be, they'd be both safer and warmer in the house.

Sydney roused herself the moment she heard the *pang* and *click* of the rear doors of the van being thrown open. As she looked up groggily, trying to get her bearings, Jack gently took the sleeping Katelyn in his arms and lifted her, still wrapped in her blanket.

Sydney sprang into action. There was, after all, still work to be done. Within minutes of their arrival in the small mountain cabin, they'd collected all of the food, water, and equipment they would require for the next few hours and set about building a small fire in the grate of the cabin's main room.

Katelyn had barely stirred as Jack placed her

on a cot in the cabin's only separate room, and closed the door between them.

"I'll do that," he said, coming upon Sydney placing some kindling around two large logs.

"No, Dad," she replied, searching her pack for some matches. "You haven't slept in almost twenty hours. I'll be fine until the extraction team gets here. You get some rest."

Jack considered his daughter and realized that there was little point in arguing, but he decided that the threadbare sofa in the corner was not nearly as inviting as the fire that was just starting to blaze up in the hearth.

He sent a coded transmission via his satellite phone to APO, and after receiving the confirmation code that indicated their extraction team was en route, he gathered the remaining food and joined his daughter on the floor beside the fire.

"They'll be here in four hours," he said, making himself as comfortable as possible. Sydney was lying on her stomach, staring into the flames. "There's a landing zone in a clearing of trees fifteen hundred meters to the north. We'll start our hike to the rendezvous point a half hour before their scheduled arrival."

He paused, examining the remaining food and selecting a handful of nuts before he attempted to make light conversation.

"Did you ever think you'd live to see the day it would be such an issue to send a team into India, where we were, but China has no problem with us compromising their air space for a mission like this?" Jack asked thoughtfully.

"China still wants things from us," Sydney replied. "India thinks they might not need us anymore."

Jack considered his daughter's blunt analysis. She was, of course, right.

"Their mistake, I'm afraid they'll find," Jack added.

Sydney rolled over onto her side, resting her head on her elbow and bringing her eyes to meet her father's. She had something on her mind. That much was obvious. Jack's instinctive response was to hide in plain sight until he had more information. Close as they'd become in the last four years, they'd faced their fair share of complex "issues." When they found themselves in disagreement, both had the tendency to defend their own positions, rather than seeking immediate compromise and reconciliation. He'd seen this solemn look in her eyes before. His gut told him that whatever was troubling her, she had already determined his most likely position and was silently seeking ways to fortify her own in the face of the impending conflict.

"What do you think will happen to Katelyn when we get back?" she asked seriously.

"To be honest, I haven't given the issue much thought," he replied neutrally.

"She's an amazing little girl," Sydney said.

"You've spent a total of six hours in her presence, and you're already sure of that?" he asked warily.

Sydney pulled herself up so that she was sitting directly across from him.

"She's not at all what I expected," she began. "Apart from her extraordinary abilities, she's a pretty normal little girl. I guess I just assumed that she'd need some sort of institutional care, but now . . . she needs a home, Dad," she finished with a hint of uncertainty.

"What is your interest or concern?" Jack asked without betraying any emotion. "For you and I, Katelyn is a mission . . . a mission we have almost accomplished. Our responsibility for her ends in four hours."

Sydney gave her father a knowing glance. "Don't worry," she replied. "I'm not considering another career change. I just . . . I need to know that she's going to be okay."

Jack softened a bit. Sydney had as big a heart as anyone he'd ever known. It wasn't hard to believe that she'd formed a tentative attachment to the girl. Katelyn's circumstances combined with her unique talents made her intriguing. Perhaps Sydney was relating too personally to the recent tragedy and upheaval of Katelyn's young life. Sydney had lost her own mother at such a young age. She'd lost two years of her life less than fourteen months ago, and gone to unimaginable lengths to get them back. She'd only recently found a measure of stability in both her work and her personal life, such as it was. It was hardly smooth sailing yet, but between the new home and the new sense of purpose she'd found with APO, she was at least within spitting distance of a life that was as close to normal as she'd had in years. Wanting the same thing for Katelyn was, in a sense, understandable. But it was also completely beyond her purview and would likely break her heart if she took too keen an interest in it.

As dispassionately as possible, Jack framed his response. "Most likely the CIA will take her into protective custody. She'll be physically and psychologically evaluated, and then suitable arrangements for her care will be made."

"What the hell does that mean?" Sydney said, her temper flaring.

"Was there a particular word you had difficulty understanding?" Jack replied peevishly.

"Physically and psychologically evaluated," Sydney spat back at him. "What you mean is they'll test her. Then, just like her father, they'll decide whether or not they can use her abilities to further their own agenda."

Jack flinched involuntarily with the harsh emphasis Sydney had placed on the words "her father." He paused, collecting his thoughts, and replied as gently as he could, "Katelyn may or may not possess the ability to take genetic engineering to an entirely new level, years before the most optimistic projections. Thousands, maybe millions, of people might benefit from her unique gifts. Are you telling me that you honestly believe that if she is capable of doing so, she should not be allowed to explore those gifts?"

"Someday . . . maybe . . . if she chooses to," Syd replied defiantly.

"With Katelyn's help Dr. Magrite went from a theoretical premise to a practical treatment for a deadly and incurable virus in less than two years, Sydney. If there are applications for her gifts in other areas, autoimmune deficiency disorders, for example, do you really think it's appropriate that millions of people continue to suffer when she might be able to offer them their lives back?"

Sydney paused. Finally she said, "She's a little girl, Dad. It's not her responsibility to cure anyone right now. What Dr. Magrite did was wrong, even though it had a positive result. He used her to further his own ends, without once considering whether or not it was right that he do so."

"How do you know he didn't consider it?" Jack replied hotly. "Just because he made the choice he did, that doesn't mean he didn't carefully weigh all of the variables. In the end he was willing to die to protect her. I think that speaks volumes about his affection and concern for her well being."

"He also said that no one should ever know what she was capable of," Sydney fired back. "Obviously he was afraid that she could be exploited by others. By turning her over to the CIA we're damning her to a life as an oddity . . . a test subject. Who is going to speak for her until she is old enough to speak for herself?"

Jack stared hard at Sydney.

"Where is this coming from?" he finally asked.

"I told you—," she started to reply.

"No," he said firmly. "This is more than a theoretical discussion or a casual interest in a relative stranger's well being."

Sydney turned her head to gaze into the fire. She didn't speak for several moments. Finally she replied, "Right now she's still got a chance. She's lost so much in the past few days, through no fault of her own, but we don't have to take her innocence from her too. Not right away." She turned her head, her pain-filled eyes reaching straight into Jack's heart and twisting it in his chest. "I know what that is, Dad. I know what it means to have your life and your choices taken away from you before you even know what's happening. I was special, wasn't I? There were certain requirements I had to have in order for you to use me as a test subject for Project Christmas, weren't there?"

It struck Jack like a sharp blow to the gut.

Oh, Sydney.

"It's true," he replied flatly. "Your cognitive abilities were tested, and your intelligence and maturity made you an ideal subject on paper. But that wasn't why I trained you to protect yourself. I was afraid—"

"I know," she interjected. "And I don't blame you for the choice you made. I'm not even sure that I care anymore whether or not that choice was the determining factor in me becoming an agent. I'm just saying, until Katelyn is old enough to make up her own mind about what she wants to do and be, we don't have the right to make that choice for her. Just because she is capable of being of use to someone, that doesn't mean we have to let her be taken advantage of. She needs to be a little girl, for as long as she can. She'll lose her innocence soon enough. Knowledge of her father's death will take some of it away, and being forced to share the rest of her childhood with strangers won't make that easier to bear. Add to that a regular regimen of appointments with men in white coats who want to treat her like a trained monkey, and she'll lose her ability to see the world with awe and wonder in no time. Innocence, once lost, is all but impossible to regain. Do we have to take that away from her too right now? All I want to know is, what can we do to make sure she's protected from all that? APO already knows, or thinks they know, what she's capable of. Once Sloane makes his report to Director Chase, that will be the end of it. Our goal should be to provide her with as normal a life as she can possibly have until she's old enough to understand what she can do and the possible benefits for society. Then it will be her choice, and believe me, if we give her the right foundation, she'll make the right one."

Jack sighed sadly. There was certainly wisdom in her argument, and logic to her fears. Unfortunately, there was also damned little he could do to prevent the most likely course of action once she was taken to the United States and placed in the hands of the various government agencies that would be entrusted with her care.

"I understand what you're saying, Sydney," Jack said softly, "but I don't think there's anything else to be done. I also honestly believe that the potential benefits of Katelyn's abilities outweigh the less tangible concerns you are raising. Have you considered the possibility that she might grow to feel as you do now? She may end up feeling that her childhood, while not ideal, did result in tremendous good. And that might provide greater peace than if she were allowed to have the childhood you're suggesting."

Sydney paused, her face hardening. Then she rose and moved to the cases of computer equipment they'd relocated from the van to protect them from the cold.

"What are you doing?" Jack asked.

He was stunned by her reply.

"I'm getting Sloane on the phone."

LOS ANGELES

Arvin Sloane was just settling into his office for the start of a new day when the emergency call came through form Lhasa. Fortifying himself against the twinge of alarm that the unplanned contact raised within him, he called up the video feed on his computer monitor and was immediately relieved when the first face he saw was Sydney's.

"Agent Bristow," he said calmly. "What can I do for you?"

Three minutes later he had digested the gist of both Sydney's and Jack's arguments. While he had no final authority to take the position that he had chosen to take less than thirty seconds into the conversation, he was certain that if handled quickly and quietly the decision he was about to make would result in little or no immediate backlash from those he answered to.

"Have you received Agent Dixon's report from Soweto?" he asked.

"No sir," Sydney replied. "Why?"

"I believe there might be an alternative before us, of which you could not be aware, that will resolve this issue to your satisfaction."

Sydney paused, her brow furrowed. The look on her face was equal parts surprise and mistrust.

Ah, Sydney, when will you understand how much you mean to me?

"Thank you," she said simply.

"Safe travels," Sloane said, ending the conversation.

When her face on the monitor had disappeared, he turned to his phone and raised his hand to press the intercom button.

Suddenly he paused.

Damn it. What the hell was that receptionist's name?

LHASA, TIBET

Jack had accepted defeat stoically and professionally, cautioning Sydney, without overemphasizing the point, that Sloane had made a surprising choice in this case. Jack suggested that she should consider all of his possible motives before celebrating prematurely. Though Sloane had not indicated exactly how he intended to facilitate Sydney's request, he had in principle agreed to honor it to the best of his abilities. Naturally, Sydney would have to satisfy herself as to whatever arrangements her demented superior had in mind, but for the time being the fact that he had not dismissed her completely nor taken Jack's side in the debate filled her with an uneasy sense of accomplishment.

Sydney did not doubt that there would be further conversation with her father at a later date about her sudden and perhaps intrusive interest in Katelyn Magrite, but for now he had retreated to the couch to catch the remaining few hours of sleep left to them.

After checking to make sure that Katelyn was still asleep in the next room, Sydney settled herself before the fire, adding another log to intensify the fire's blaze and ensure their relative comfort for the final hours of their stay in the safe house.

The next sound she was conscious of was both disorienting and disturbing. Jarred into sudden alertness, she sat straight up and noted first that her father was snoring softly on the couch.

Must have been my imagination, she thought, shaking herself awake and trying to get her bearings in the darkness. The fire had burned to little more than a few embers, and the room was much colder than it had been when she dozed off. She didn't punish herself too harshly for having drifted into semiconsciousness. Given the last two days, she was mentally and physically approaching exhaustion. Nonetheless, she knew her father was only sleeping so peacefully because he trusted her to remain vigilant. She was crossing as softly as she could to the hearth, intent on rebuilding the fire, when she heard it again.

The unmistakable whir of a helicopter flying low, and approaching from the south.

She was immediately wide awake. Checking her watch, she confirmed what the pit in her gut and the tingling of her nerve endings already told her to be true. They were still an hour away from their pickup time. The reality washing over her sent dozens of unsettling thoughts rushing to the front of her mind, demanding priority.

But only one was crystal clear.

She rushed to her father's side and shook him firmly.

His eyes shot open, and the words "What is it?" were out of his mouth before he bothered to sit up.

"We have company," Sydney whispered in the darkness.

He was immediately on his feet.

"The extraction team?" he asked.

"Not unless they're an hour early," she replied.

He paused to listen. The helicopter was back, circling the house. They locked eyes for a moment, their most pressing needs communicated clearly between them in the silence.

"It won't take them long to find the landing zone. We have half an hour, no more, before they're here," he diagnosed.

His first action was to begin grabbing their

gear. Before he was out the door for his first run to the van, Sydney stopped him.

"We can't run," she said simply.

"Yes, we can," he replied.

"No." She shook her head. "We can't."

"Can we discuss this in the van?" he asked sharply.

"That has to be Gupta's men," Sydney said very calmly. "They're not looking for us because they're pissed. They're looking for us because they know the truth about Katelyn. Otherwise, there's no way they'd expend the resources to track us here. If they have the faintest inkling of what she can do, they're not going to rest until they've found her or she's dead."

Jack paused, obviously understanding the gravity of her words.

"We'll redirect the extraction team. We'll be out of the country in two hours. Then they can look all they want for all the good it will do them," he replied.

"No, that won't be enough," Sydney said sharply. She crossed to her father, placing a gentle hand on his arm.

"Project Christmas," she said softly.

"I thought we'd settled that," he replied.

"Why did you train me to protect myself?" she said earnestly.

"Because I knew I couldn't always be there to protect you myself," he replied honestly.

"I know," she said, and nodded, smiling faintly. "I do understand, in a way I never have before. As long as Katelyn is alive, Gupta, or men like him, will be after her. You know as well as I do how often our intelligence and secrets are compromised. They'll find her, and they'll force her to do whatever they ask. Even the best protective custody can't prevent that. And we can't teach her to protect herself."

"What do you suggest?" Jack asked.

"First, we need to contact our extraction team," she replied.

CHAPTER 10

LHASA, TIBET

Faster . . .

Must . . . go . . . faster!

Katelyn was roughly a hundred meters ahead of her. Sydney had to close some of that distance in the next fifteen seconds. Normally that wouldn't have been a problem, but there were two things working against her right now.

One was the terrain. She'd been forced to choose between the open path to the north of the house, which meandered down the hill in a gentle slope, or the more densely wooded area she was now flying through as fast as she could.

The problem with the first choice had been simple. If their pursuers had any sense at all, and she didn't doubt they did, they'd have chosen to land on the natural rise to the north that APO had already designated as their landing zone. It was clear of trees for eighty meters in any direction, as if Mother Nature had decided that at some point in the future she would be installing a helipad of her own, or perhaps an Olympic-size pool. So while the open path would have been easier to traverse, it would also have made Sydney and Katelyn more vulnerable to encountering those who were after them.

The rocky tree-filled forest they were currently making their way through ran east-southeast from the safe house and ended in a steeper and more treacherous trail which led to the valley below. Despite the low-hanging branches and the occasional patches of ice, it was still the more attractive choice from a tactical point of view. The trees provided natural cover, and Gupta's men would be facing the same obstacle course as Syd, Jack, and Katelyn. All other things being equal, Syd knew the timing would be crucial. She hoped her team's slight but decisive lead would be enough.

It hadn't been that difficult choice at the time. But Sydney had not factored in challenge number two, which was that Katelyn was the fastest eleven-year-old sprinter she'd ever seen. Her height protected her from all but the lowest of branches, and she ran with a sure-footed grace that Sydney found herself envying.

Shots rang out behind her.

Dad.

She was closing on Katelyn, but not as quickly as she would have liked. Jack had given them a good head start. They'd waited at the tree line until they'd caught their first glimpse of the six-man team trudging toward the safe house, equipped with cold-weather gear and automatic weapons. Only when all three were sure they had been spotted had Katelyn been given the nod to go. Sydney followed moments later. Jack would have taken his first clear shot, but he was armed only with a handgun. From a distance where he would have felt safe, an accurate shot would have been a problem, even for as amazing a marksman as her father. At any rate the shots were the signal she'd been waiting for. Every second counted now.

This is going to be close.

Jack's estimate that it would take the men in the helicopter thirty minutes to find them had been optimistic. Though they'd spent wisely the twenty minutes they ended up with, Sydney would have preferred one more practice run before the actual show.

Her left foot skidded forward, causing her to lose a moment of forward momentum. She surged forward and righted herself, at the same time painfully aware of an unpleasant give in her left ankle.

Katelyn's bright pink sneakers were barely visible now.

Syd forced herself to ignore the pain, and she found new reserves of adrenaline coursing through her veins. She was rewarded seconds later with her first clear sight of Katleyn's back since their dash into the snowy forest had commenced.

The edge of the cliff was a hundred meters away.

TWENTY MINUTES EARLIER

"Katelyn," Sydney whispered, every nerve in her body tingling with hyperalertness even as she tried to keep her voice as calm as possible.

Katelyn roused herself slowly, and when she saw Sydney's face next to her own, she smiled in recognition.

"Are we where it's warm yet?" she asked sleepily.

"No," Sydney replied more sharply than she'd intended. At Katelyn's faintly furrowed brow, she forced her own face to relax, and continued in a hurried whisper, "I want you to come with me."

"What's wrong?" Katelyn asked.

"Nothing," Sydney said, and shook her head. "We're going to play a game. After that we'll go straight to the warm place . . . I promise."

Katelyn considered Sydney appraisingly, then started to sit up.

"What kind of game?" she asked.

Moments later they'd made their way into the living room. The fire had been put out. Certainly by now Gupta's men had seen the smoke curling from the chimney, but there was no reason to make this too easy for them.

Sydney knew that all CIA safe houses were equipped with a broad range of gear designed for multiple rescue scenarios. She'd made use of them time and time again in her career. Her entire plan hinged on the presence of at least one specially designed parachute, and she'd almost wept with relief when she'd found the parachute nestled in among ammunition, battery operated lights, and the few handguns they'd been provided with.

The chute in question was actually a model that had been designed, at least in part, by APO's own Marshall. When SD-6 had still been operating and Marshall had been their resident tech expert, he'd designed the safety chute to fit into an incredibly small pouch that could be sewn seamlessly into a normal jacket. Because he was being sent on his first flight and was absolutely terrified of flying, he'd created several for himself, and the one that most closely resembled an average brown blazer had managed to save both his life and Sydney's.

The jacket stored at the safe house was not nearly as well tailored, but it more than suited Sydney's purposes. While her father had redirected the extraction team to a point in the valley less than two miles away from their intended destination, and apprised them of Sydney's plan, she had rigged the chute's release with a small remote activator. This would allow her to control, from a distance of ten meters at the most, when the chute opened, since she had no intention of actually wearing it.

Getting Katelyn to wear it proved more daunting a task than she'd anticipated.

"But it's black," Katelyn pouted.

Sydney considered the pink denim jacket the child was currently wearing, which was covered with patches of roses on the sleeves, and in a flashback to her own adolescence Sydney remembered how important such things had been to her. For someone like Katelyn, who experienced colors in ways that Sydney could appreciate but not fully understand, it would be even more important.

This could be a problem.

"I know," Sydney finally said. "But it's also magic."

Katelyn shot her a look that would have dissolved her into fits of laughter under any other circumstances.

"Real magic?" she asked reproachfully.

"Of course!" Sydney replied.

Glancing down at Katelyn's tennis shoes, Sydney added, "And you still have your pink sneakers. They're going to be very important too because there is a lot of running in this game."

Katelyn's face brightened. She looked down at her shoes, lifted one foot to its toe and spun it inward to really enjoy the view, then said almost challengingly, "I happen to be a very fast runner."

Sydney didn't even try to repress her smile. "Good," she replied. "Me too."

Once she'd satisfied herself that the interior harness of the jacket was cinched firmly over Katelyn's shoulders and around her thighs, Sydney zipped up the front to hide the internal chute. She had no intention of letting Gupta's men get close enough to see what was hidden behind that zipper, but you couldn't be too careful.

"So how does this game work?" Katelyn asked as they shuffled out onto the porch. Sydney cast a sharp eye around the side of the house. It was still at least fifteen minutes until their pursuers would reach the crest of the hill, but she couldn't afford to take any chances.

"It's really simple," Sydney told her as they made their way down the front steps. "You're going to run as fast as you can toward the edge of the hill, and at the last minute you're going to jump forward as far as you can."

"And what's the magic part?" Katelyn asked seriously.

"When you jump, instead of falling . . . you're going to fly," Sydney replied, infusing as much suspense and excitement into her voice as she could.

Katelyn's eyes grew wide.

"You're not afraid, are you?" Sydney asked.

Katelyn studied her closely for a moment, then shook her head.

"Good," Sydney said. "I'm going to be right behind you. I promise, as long as you jump really far . . . as far as you can . . . you'll be flying in no time."

Katelyn stepped back. With both feet planted on the ground she hefted herself into the air and fell forward into a soft mound of snow only three feet in front of her.

"That's pretty good," Sydney said, "but you'll go a lot farther if you give yourself a running start."

Sydney helped Katelyn up and brushed her off. "You ready to try it again?"

Katelyn nodded, her face a mask of determination.

"Okay," Sydney said. "Let's run together to that rock over there, and when we get to the rock, we'll both jump and see who jumps farther."

Katelyn took off without warning. Sydney barely managed to catch her at the rock. But this time, as Sydney had promised, Katelyn cleared at least nine feet before she skidded to the ground, landing this time on her backside.

"Are you okay?" Sydney asked, crawling to her from her own landing spot a few feet farther than Katelyn's.

But the girl was already standing up, saying, "I can do better."

Sydney looked at her with mock seriousness and said, "I don't know . . . that was pretty far."

Five jumps later Sydney was satisfied that Katelyn had the muscle memory she would need. After congratulating her heartily for her efforts, she said, "Okay, now I'm going to show you the place you're actually going to jump from. Ready?"

Katelyn nodded enthusiastically and followed Sydney into the forest, running a little ahead and challenging Sydney to keep up.

Sydney was pleased that once they'd reached the bend in the trail that jutted sharply down the side of the hill, and she'd pointed out the spot from which Katelyn should launch herself, Katelyn didn't change her mind about the game. Perhaps it was a blessing that she trusted Sydney so implicitly, and that she didn't seem to doubt for a moment that the magic Sydney had promised her would work. Sydney knew it would, but convincing most eleven-year-olds of that in this day and age would have been all but impossible. At any rate she was able to clearly point out the ledge where Katelyn would land just below the drop if she didn't jump as far as she could. Katelyn took this as the challenge it was and assured Sydney that she was up to it.

She was ready to fly.

They made their way back to the cabin more slowly. Katelyn didn't seem to be too weary, but knowing what was to come, Sydney didn't want to push her too hard.

As they walked, Katelyn seemed to really take in their surroundings. She commented on the occasional tree or rock, and Sydney had to work a little to encourage her to move along. Fascinating as the "yellow" rock and "red" branch were, they didn't have time to really enjoy what would have otherwise been a fascinating experience.

When they were once again in sight of the cabin, Katelyn paused, her eyes downcast. Sensing the change, Sydney knelt before her and asked, "Are you okay?"

Katelyn traced a small circle in the snow with the tip of her shoe, then asked, "Are you going to fly too?"

Sydney considered her response carefully. Finally she said, "Only pink little girls get to fly. Silver and gold girls are the ones who make the magic happen."

Katelyn's eyes brightened. "You think I'm pink?"

Sydney paused. It hadn't really occurred to her that Katelyn wouldn't have chosen this, her happiest color, for herself.

"Definitely." She nodded firmly.

The little girl smiled. "I can't tell about me. I like pink. I want to be pink. But even when I look in the mirror and count everything there is to count, the numbers don't show me my color."

"Well, I see pink," Sydney replied, once again drawing the little girl into a fierce hug.

At that moment Jack emerged from the front door onto the porch of the safe house. He gestured for Sydney to hurry toward him as he began to close the distance quickly from his side as well.

"What is it?" she asked, doing her best to hide

the fear that the concern on his face had aroused in her.

"They're coming up the hill now," he replied tensely. "We have two minutes. No more."

Sydney nodded, then pulled her father a few meters away.

"Just so we're clear . . . they have to see this."

"I understand," he replied, then offered her a tight smile.

"Okay," Sydney said.

"You realize all of this will be more convincing if you appear to be visibly upset when—," Jack started.

"Don't worry about that," Sydney cut him off. Glancing at Katelyn, who was busy retying the laces on her bright pink shoes, her voice softened as she answered his unspoken question. "Either way, I'm never going to see her again. Not like this, anyway."

Jack nodded in understanding. As they both turned their attention to the cabin, watching for the first sign of Gupta's men, he placed a gentle arm around her shoulder. A moment later Katelyn joined them, tugging gently at Sydney's sleeve. She looked up at her, her blue eyes dancing, and said, "So when do we start . . . for real?"

ONE HUNDRED METERS FROM THE EDGE

As Sydney put on an extra burst of speed, she thought she saw Katelyn falter. Sydney had to be within ten meters of the little girl when she launched herself off the cliff, and at this rate she wasn't absolutely certain she could close the distance in time.

Katelyn's head ducked out of sight as Sydney quickly made up thirty yards. Just to be sure, Sydney carried the remote trigger in her right hand, her thumb wrapped safely around the side of the handle so as not to risk depressing the release early or inadvertently.

The next clear sight she had, Katelyn was up again and running, though perhaps a little slower than before.

What happened? Sydney gave herself a moment to wonder. She wanted to call out, but she didn't, for fear that Katelyn would stop and return, wondering if the rules of the game had changed.

Then she learned the hard way what had slowed Katelyn momentarily. Running at full speed, Sydney felt her left foot find a depression in the snow, a dip that was covered by soft powder that would not hold her weight. Katelyn had weakened it in her passage, possibly stumbling in the process. Sydney's foot dropped a full two feet into the crevice, and at the speed she had taken it, she heard—even before she felt—a sharp crack. It was too soon to tell, but it certainly felt broken.

"KATELYN!" Sydney screamed without thinking.

Oh, no.

Sydney had a clear sight of Katelyn approaching the tree line. If she didn't stop and Sydney couldn't reach her in time . . .

Sydney rose from the crouched position where she'd fallen, and surged forward. A clatter of gunfire rattled in the distance, but that distance was getting shorter and shorter each second.

Her left foot shot spikes of burning pain up her leg, which resonated in her teeth every other step, but she refused to heed it.

The little pink shoes cleared the tree line. There were less than twenty yards now between Katelyn and death.

Tears of pain, frustration, and terror burst forth from Sydney's eyes as she screamed again, "KATELYN!"

Faster! Every cell of Sydney's body cried out in alarm.

Sydney was still ten meters from the tree line. Her body demanded that she stop. Heaven only knew how much additional damage she was inflicting on herself as she continued her mad dash forward. But she didn't care. Only one thing mattered now.

Katelyn was five meters from the edge. True to her training, she did not hesitate. Fifteen meters behind her, Sydney watched in horror as the little girl sprang forward, just as she'd practiced, and hurled herself off the cliff . . . waiting for the magic.

Sydney closed the last few meters. Fifteen meters became ten. She could do this. But with each millisecond, gravity was pulling Katelyn farther and farther away.

Sydney threw herself forward at the last second, breaking her fall and skidding to a stop at the cliff's edge. As she did so, she moved her thumb and with a silent prayer activated the remote chute.

Then the screams began.

Katelyn had dreamed many nights of flying. She hadn't told the beautiful silver and gold girl about her dreams, but one of the reasons she was so excited about the game was that she knew in dreams that you could fly forever and ever.

She hadn't been afraid when she jumped. The magic was real. It had to be. The girl would not have lied to her. She was not capable of lying about something as important as magic. Katelyn had seen it in her eyes.

Katelyn did her part, jumping as far from the edge of the cliff as she could.

That was a good jump!

But instead of stretching out and soaring like a bird, like she did in her dreams, she found herself falling . . . down and down into the blackness.

She heard herself screaming.

Suddenly she wanted the game to end. She wanted her daddy and her aunt Ceci and the roses and the children whose colors didn't make sense.

Then she remembered what the girl had told her on their last journey through the forest.

"Katelyn," the beautiful girl had said, "the minute you jump I want you to start counting."

She could do that.

"What am I supposed to count?" she had asked.

"Whatever you like," the girl had replied. "Count the stars."

"And when will the magic happen?" she had asked next.

"Before you get to ten."

Katelyn had managed to count three hundred forty-seven points of light before she was suddenly falling . . . differently.

Instead of feeling like she was being drawn down like a magnet, she suddenly felt light. Slow.

Looking up, she realized that floating above her was a bright white canopy.

The magic.

Her screams became tickles. The feeling she had only known before in her dreams became part of her waking world. She glided down and down, drifting on the magic, and found herself wanting to count more stars . . . wanting to count all of the stars in the sky so that the magic would never end.

She had reached seven hundred eighty-six when it dawned on her that she had never asked the beautiful silver and gold girl her name. She wanted to make a file on her computer at home and call it—

But she didn't know what to call it.

This thought troubled her so that she stopped

counting. She thought of all the colors she had seen in the girl, her brilliant gleaming that was so bright it was almost blinding, and the magic the beautiful girl had given her that allowed her to fly.

Bright bird.

Then she had it.

Phoenix.

The screams echoed on and on. Suddenly the pain in her leg and the pain in her heart were one, and deep inside, Sydney began to howl in anguish.

But the cries wouldn't come out. Battering them down was a voice that demanded she crawl farther out and check to see if Katelyn's chute had opened. But she couldn't. She sat there, frozen between fear and hope, only conscious of the pain.

Each time she tried to nudge herself forward, she was blinded by the color pink. She couldn't see past it, and didn't want to.

Suddenly her father was beside her.

"Get up!" he shouted.

Why? part of her mind wondered.

"Sydney, get up!" he said more forcefully, grabbing her shoulder with his free hand as he sprayed the figures emerging from the tree line with the last remaining bullets in his Beretta.

Tears streaming down her face, her leg a riot of fiery nerve endings, Sydney suddenly realized what she had to do.

Pink became red.

Grasping her father's arm, she rose where she had fallen and pulled out her 9mm just as Jack replaced the clip in his Beretta.

As they began to fire at the four men who had made it through the forest, the tide of the battle turned. Sydney realized with grim satisfaction that at least this much of her plan had worked. Two of their attackers, two who had seen Katelyn jump and heard the screams, now believed what Sydney had wanted them to believe.

The little girl they had chased all this way was dead.

Rather than face the fury that Sydney and Jack were raining down upon them, Sydney watched as they turned tail and retreated into the forest.

The other two were down before they had a chance to reach the same conclusion.

Sydney stood panting at the cliff's edge, her breath coming in spasms of white air as her father grabbed her firmly under her left arm, supporting the foot that he could now clearly see dangling, useless, from her left leg.

"Well done," he gasped through pants of his own.

Sydney managed a weak shake of her head.

"What is it?" Jack asked with sudden concern. "I mean, apart from the obvious?"

"I didn't . . . I don't think I . . ." But she couldn't even say the words.

Jack reached for Sydney's right hand. The remote activator was equipped with a flip-panel display that indicated the chute's status. He popped the panel open and saw, just as he'd certainly expected, that the signal had remained constant long enough to open Katelyn's parachute.

He raised the release to Sydney's face and put an end to the nightmare for her.

Overwhelmed with relief, Sydney threw herself into her father's arms and wept as she hadn't allowed herself to for months, her sobs pouring out into the darkness until their echoes died out among the countless stars that filled the sky.

* * *

Below, Vaughn and Dixon watched as their tacticians disentangled Katelyn from her parachute. Vaughn knew that somewhere up above, Sydney was fighting for her life. His heart told him that she would survive. The sudden change of plan meant that a separate team had been dispatched to the original drop zone, to clear out any stragglers Gupta's men might have left behind and to rendezvous with Jack and Sydney. A separate carrier, their backup for this mission, would arrive shortly, but rather than being reunited with Sydney tonight, as he'd hoped, he still wouldn't see her for several more hours.

Sydney had made a personal request of him, that he watch over Katelyn for the duration of the girl's trip back to the States. He'd agreed readily, unsure as to why this was so important to her but nonetheless more than willing to do anything that would put her mind at ease.

Once Katelyn was free, he moved quickly toward her. She was staring up at the sky, her face lit by a bright smile. Kneeling before her, he asked, "Are you okay?"

She turned her smile on him and said, "Can I do it again? Oh, please?"

Vaughn smiled. Whatever spell she had cast

over Sydney was instantly taking effect on him as well.

"I'll tell you what," he replied, "we'll go back up in the air, and I'll make sure you get a window seat. Do you know what that is?"

Katelyn shook her head.

"How about I show you?"

Katelyn studied him carefully for a moment, her face inscrutable. Then it brightened a bit as she whispered, "Red . . . that wants to be bright white."

Suddenly Vaughn's earpiece crackled to life.

"Phoenix to Shotgun."

"Go ahead, Phoenix," Vaughn replied softly.

"Is the package secured?"

"Affirmative," he replied.

After a pause, Sydney's voice fell almost to a whisper as she said, "Thank you."

Vaughn lifted Katelyn into his arms, and as they made their way toward the waiting helicopter, she said, "Phoenix . . . I know her."

"You do?" Vaughn asked, unsure if they could really be talking about the same person.

Katelyn nodded seriously. "She wants to be bright white too."

"What does that mean?" Vaughn asked.

Katelyn explained it to him over the next several hours. In the end Vaughn realized she couldn't have been more right.

CHAPTER 11

LOS ANGELES

The next morning Sydney had almost reached the conference room when Marshall tugged gently on her sleeve and motioned her into his office.

"How's the foot?" he asked thoughtfully as he pulled up a stool for her to sit on.

Realizing that she was still favoring it with each step, but relieved that a full examination had revealed a serious sprain but no break, Sydney eased herself onto the stool and replied, "Better, thanks."

"I thought you should see this," Marshall said,

pulling up a screen on his monitor that showed a strand of DNA with color-coded genes and dozens of calculations that were indecipherable to her.

"What is it?" she asked.

"I've spent the last twenty-eight hours breaking down the vectors Katelyn created for her father's patients," he replied enthusiastically.

"Really?" Sydney said, truly interested.

"Yeah . . . it's . . . okay . . . my brain . . . seriously fried . . . but in a good way, you know?"

Sydney nodded encouragingly.

"I mean, I can't do what she did. I don't know who could. But . . . at the same time, I wanted to just sit down with her and, you know, dump everything I could out of her head and into mine. . . . I was thinking . . . she's just a kid, leave her alone. So I figured, next best thing . . . let's do as much of it as we can . . . ourselves. 'Cause, you know, it's our job."

Sydney smiled warmly.

Leave it to Marshall to understand.

"So I've run all of the successful vectors through analysis, and while there are certain discrepancies I can't really account for, there are also a number of commonalities that you don't really see unless you run the numbers."

"What does that mean?" Sydney asked.

"Well, I'm not saying, you know, today . . . but I think we have enough information here to at least pass on to our researchers . . . okay . . . once they've been Flinkmaned—the information, not the researchers. That would be . . . Well, Carrie would not approve."

Sydney couldn't help but interject. "'Flinkmaned'? Really? That's what we're calling it now?"

"I don't know," Marshall said uncertainly. "You think 'Flinkmanized' sounds better?"

When Sydney couldn't muster a reply, he went on, "Point is, there's a lot of really valuable stuff here. And the potential applications are . . . huge."

"Marshall," Sydney asked, "are you saying that you can do what Katelyn did . . . without her?"

"Not exactly. I mean, she's . . . even more of a freak of nature than I am. But I've started a new program that will take what she did and break it down in a way that, given a little more work, might lead us to the same place she can just, you know . . . go to. We're kind of working backward, but still, it gives us a much more solid place to start. Basically we're talking about large numbers and theoretical equations that . . . I don't want to bore you, but . . ."

Sydney stood and took Marshall by the shoulders. Smiling, she kissed him gently on the cheek and then enveloped him in a hug.

"Thank you," she said softly.

"Sure," he replied uncertainly. Releasing her, he added, "Just . . . you know . . . doing my job."

"Good work, everyone," Sloane said as he entered the briefing room. Jack cast a quick glance at Sydney, who was seated directly across from him. She seemed pleased, or at the very least relieved. Few despised praise from Sloane more than Jack, but Sydney could be counted on that very short list.

Vaughn was seated on Sydney's right, while Dixon and Marshall sat opposite Sloane, who had taken a seat at the head of the table.

"Despite Dr. Magrite's tragic death, I want to commend you all on the safe return of his daughter, Katelyn. Thanks to your skill and dedication she can now look forward to a long, happy, and much safer life," he said, nodding meaningfully at Sydney.

Jack had already thoroughly reviewed the debriefing packet Sloane had provided each of them. Apart from indicating that Katelyn had survived her ordeal with a minimum of trauma, it remained stubbornly vague as to her current whereabouts or as to arrangements for her future.

"We have also managed to uncover the identity of the designer of the Marburg strain, and you will no doubt be pleased to know that Surgit Gupta and several of Proto-Chem's directors, who were aware of his activities, have all been taken into custody. It looks as if Gupta is trying to arrange for some sort of leniency in return for providing intel about many of those he dealt with on a regular basis," Sloane went on.

"Why not? It's all the rage." Jack heard Sydney whisper to Vaughn. His face cracked a millimeter of a smile. Though Sloane's use of the imperial "we" in referencing the work that Sydney, Vaughn, Dixon, Marshall, and Jack had accomplished over the past three days was galling, it was certainly par for the course, as was Sydney's reflexive inability to cut him any slack at all. Jack had worried after her somewhat overemotional, and to his mind inappropriate, call to Sloane to intercede on Katelyn's behalf that Sydney might actually be softening to APO's head of operations. Her comment seemed to indicate otherwise, and that was good enough for now.

"Gupta's first act as a reformed citizen was to

provide us with the location of the plant where the Marburg strain and several other biological agents were in development," Sloane continued.

When a slide came up on the room's main monitor, Jack briefly studied the aerial image of what had once been a large stone building on a deserted road. The structural carcass had a strangely antiseptic look. The team sent in to demolish the lab had probably taken most of it apart brick by brick in their efforts to safely and appropriately deal with yet another threat to the world's safety.

"Has Gupta given any reason for his sudden change of heart?" Dixon asked. "Surely he's not being offered a plea?"

"No," Sloane replied curtly. "He will not receive the death penalty for his actions, but he will never again walk the earth as a free man. As to the first question, it seems his son has somewhat miraculously recovered from the Marburg infection that set off this entire chain of events. Sayteesh Gupta has also been taken into custody, but the reports of his recovery are quite encouraging. He appears to have been one of the lucky few who have some sort of inborn immunity to the disease. Though he suffered terribly, his condition was eventually stabilized, much to his father's surprise."

"What about Magrite's patients in Tshwane?" Vaughn asked.

"Those Dr. Magrite was able to treat before his abduction are all doing very well. A small percentage of the others infected also survived, but it saddens me to report that, in all, Gupta's attack on Tshwane resulted in forty-seven deaths."

Sloane took a brief moment of silence before concluding by saying, "Finally, Marshall has begun some preliminary work on Katelyn Magrite's files, which we are hopeful will allow us at some point to recreate what she has done and significantly diminish the threat of another such attack."

Jack allowed most of his mind to zone out to Sloane's remaining few comments. Everything he needed to know about the mission was contained in the final reports he had at his fingertips. Sloane's congratulations were completely beside the point.

Turning his attention again to Sydney, he watched as she favored Marshall with a bright smile. It was good to see her happy, especially after riding the highs and lows of the past few days with her. What he wished for her, however, went beyond happiness.

Far too many people set the same amorphous

goal for themselves and spent a lifetime chasing something they could never have because of a simple lack of specificity. Happiness was far too vague a feeling. He couldn't remember the last time he'd felt or even desired to feel anything so utterly ridiculous. Serenity, rapture, centeredness, completion, satisfaction . . . these words captured part of it.

But no.

As he considered his precious daughter's face and reflected on the troubles she'd left behind—and the dark and ever-shifting road that lay before her—what he wanted most of all was something no one, least of all he, could ever give her. It was something she was going to have to find for herself.

What Jack wished for Sydney was peace.

As the meeting adjourned, Michael looked to Sydney to ask whether or not she would be free to spend the rest of the day with him. Before he had a chance to catch her eye, however, loud and good-natured greetings were directed toward APO's two previously absent agents, Nadia and Weiss.

Apart from half a dozen cell phone messages that had been waiting in Vaughn's mailbox when he'd returned, and which Vaughn hadn't had the energy to listen to, he'd had no direct contact with Eric since his little "holiday" with Nadia had begun.

For her part Nadia appeared vibrant and well rested. The same sun that had turned her faintly brown skin a soft golden tone had not, it seemed, looked as kindly on Eric. Though there were wide stark-white ovals around his eyes—*sunglasses,* Vaughn realized with an internal chuckle—his cheeks and high forehead were a bright and clearly painful shade of red.

"How was your week, my friend?" Vaughn asked, shaking Eric's hand hello.

"Good," Weiss replied with an impish grin. "Two things, though," he continued, "did you change your cell phone number, or were you too busy saving the world to help out a friend?"

Vaughn smiled in spite of himself. This was clearly a rhetorical question.

"Also . . . just curious . . . those people who make SPF sixty, are they kidding? Because I'm living proof that they're either liars or don't know how to do fractions. Ninety-eight percent blockage, my ass."

"So you had a good time?" Vaughn asked.

Weiss checked the immediate vicinity to make sure no one would overhear, before he leaned in to say, "You should have checked those messages."

Vaughn turned to grab Sydney, expecting to see her catching up with her half sister, but he realized she had left the room. Puzzled, he checked the hall, which was partially visible through the room's windows, and saw her slipping into Sloane's office.

He was about to go after her when Nadia appeared before him, smiling brightly and offering him a brief hug.

"It's good to see you," she said sweetly. "How's Sydney?"

"Hey, hey," Weiss said, stepping between them. "Just remember, I'm the one who paid for the—"

"Sunscreen?" Vaughn cut him off.

"Very funny," Weiss replied.

"Have you ever been to Palm Springs?" Nadia asked in an obvious effort to change the subject.

"Yeah," Vaughn replied, "but it's been a while."

"It's beautiful there," she continued.

"Yeah," Weiss interjected, stone-faced. "It's a dry heat."

As they fell into an easy banter, Vaughn smiled inwardly to see that at least so far things were going well between the new couple.

"So, what'd we miss?" Weiss finally asked.

Vaughn paused, then replied, "Not much. Just, you know, making the world safe for—"

"Yeah, yeah, yeah," Weiss broke in. "Seriously, how are things going with you and Syd?"

"Why do you ask?" Vaughn retorted.

"I don't know," he replied. "Things just seem a little—what's the word? Cold, maybe?"

"We're not cold," Vaughn said, shaking his head slightly. "What makes you say that?"

"Nothing . . . just—So, Palm Springs! You have to go with us sometime. Don't you think, Nadia? Don't you think Vaughn and Syd would love it there? There's this great little Italian place on the main drag. What was that place called?"

Vaughn brushed aside Weiss's obvious attempt to change the subject. "Just how much of your vacation did you spend vacationing and how much did you spend talking about stuff that's none of your business?" he asked.

"I'm your best friend and Nadia is Syd's sister. What are the odds that it didn't come up?" Eric replied.

"Well, knock it off," Vaughn said.

"Yeah, that's going to happen," Weiss said, and chuckled.

* * *

Sydney hadn't really planned to follow Sloane into his office once the briefing ended. First there was the fact that more than a few moments in his presence still tended to sour her stomach. More important, however, was that she had been rethinking her impulsive call to him the previous day.

She didn't like to go over anyone's head, particularly her father's. She would if the situation absolutely required it, but those times had always been few and far between. Most often, she reasoned, if she couldn't frame an argument compelling enough to win someone on the other side of an issue, that was usually an indication that she needed to rethink her premise. In addition it felt wrong to have put herself under Sloane's power by choice, to have acknowledged his ability to solve a problem of hers. She had decided weeks ago, when she'd accepted her assignment to the APO team, that she would do her work with grace and professionalism, but there was no bridge in the world large enough to have washed under all of the water that stood between herself and Sloane.

If at the end of the day, however, Sydney's action resulted in a better life for Katelyn, maybe the sacrifice had been worth it. Or maybe, as her father often pointed out to her, she had once again allowed her emotional response to a situation to cloud her judgment. It wasn't that she would have preferred to see Katelyn live the next several years of her life under a microscope. But it truly hadn't been her place to demand what she had demanded.

Of course, the question that was really troubling her was, Why had Sloane agreed with her? Did he honestly share her feelings? Or was this part of some larger agenda he was working on? Time would tell, but in the short-term she needed to satisfy herself that she hadn't lost too much of the higher ground by doing what she'd done.

So, with a dull sensation in the pit of her stomach, she made her way quietly out of the conference room and found herself tapping lightly on the door frame of Sloane's office.

"Oh . . . Sydney," he said, smiling faintly once he'd looked up. "Come in. Oh, and close the door, would you?"

Ick.

At least she knew she could take him.

Sloane had been writing something on a notepad as she'd entered. He completed the task, tore the paper from the pad, and folded it in his hand as he approached her and gestured for her to sit opposite him on the couch.

How to begin?

"I guess I just wanted to thank you—," she started.

Sloane waived her off, eliminating the need for her to finish the thought.

"There's no need," he said graciously. "You're no doubt worried that I might feel I did you some sort of favor in regards to Katelyn Magrite?" he asked.

"Actually, I am," she replied coolly, meeting his even gaze.

"Well, don't be," he replied. "I do not allow myself the luxury of illusions anymore. If there is anywhere on record a tally of the things I owe you versus the things you owe me, I am acutely aware of whose list is longer. I meant what I said last year when I told you, and in many ways you and your father are my penance and my only hope for redemption. I don't intend to squander the opportunity that joining APO has provided for me. And I'm certain you will make me live up to that every day we are fortunate enough to work together."

As usual, Sloane's little speech left Sydney cold.

It had been a long time since his words had held the promise of anything but manipulative calculation, despite the warmth with which they were delivered.

"I'm glad to hear that," was all Sydney could muster and still maintain a facade of politeness.

"And I think you should know," Sloane went on, "in this instance, I happen to agree with you. I think for too many years of my life I confused power with morality. Once I realized what I could do, I stopped asking myself whether or not that also meant I *should*. Emily's death, my discovery of Nadia . . . they've once again forced me to look at myself and ask harder questions than I used to pose. In the case of Katelyn Magrite, I could easily understand your vehemence on the subject, but I also found myself drawn toward your conclusions. No human being is made solely for the use of another. The gifts Katelyn has been blessed with, they are hers to use as she will. No one, least of all an organization, even one dedicated to the good, should take those choices away from her."

Tentatively relieved, Sydney started to rise as she replied, "Good, then."

Impulsively Sloane grabbed her right hand and added, "Of course, I would be lying if I didn't tell you that the most decisive factor in my decision was that *you* were the one asking. I never thought you would come to me again, seeking my counsel or making any kind of serious personal request. You could have demanded it, after all. You could have threatened me with any number of unpleasant scenarios. But you didn't. You simply asked. I want you to know, Sydney, that I really do hope that this can be a fresh start for all of us, but particularly for you and me. There is really almost nothing I wouldn't do for you, Sydney. You know that, don't you?"

With that, he rose, released her hand, and crossed toward the door. "Now, if you'll excuse me, I have a meeting with Director Chase," he said simply, and left.

Once he had gone, Sydney allowed the wave of nausea that always accompanied these little heart-to-heart chats to pass. It took a full minute of slow measured breathing and firm mental reminders that the ends did justify the means, before she could focus herself and walk calmly from the room.

She had reached her desk before she realized that when Sloane had taken her hand, he had passed her the note he'd been writing when she entered. Written in his familiar scrawl was an address.

EPILOGUE

Sydney didn't know exactly what had prompted her decision to include Vaughn on her little trip. She had guessed, or hoped, she knew the location to which Sloane had directed her. Part of her felt she would be compromising something, maybe just Katelyn's safety, by asking Vaughn to join her. But part of her also wanted him there. It wasn't a question of trust. Trust was no longer an issue between them. It was more a question of how he would react to the choice she had made.

Though they had spent several hours curled in

bed the night before, their first night back together, talking in soft whispers about the little girl and the extraordinary way her mind worked, Sydney hadn't told Michael about the conversation she'd had with her father and Sloane. She wasn't ashamed of it. She just didn't want to question it anymore, and though she believed Michael would have agreed with her, she wasn't absolutely certain he would have been thrilled with the means she had used to secure Katelyn's safety.

He had expressed his own fears for Katelyn. He, too, had seen immediately how dangerous and decisive a weapon the little girl could become in the hands of an enemy. But he had also seen how difficult her life could become in the hands of the government now entrusted with her care. He'd let the matter drop when they discussed how Sydney had revealed her code name, Phoenix, to Katelyn. After racking her brain, Sydney had been unable to think of an instance when it had come up between them. She hadn't been at liberty to tell Katelyn her real name, much as she would have liked to. Finally she decided Katelyn must have overheard it somehow in the hours they'd spent in the van or the cabin.

In the silence that followed, a pleasant comfortable quiet as they both drifted toward sleep, Sydney had finally remembered that she and Vaughn needed to talk about *them.* But somehow, in all that she'd been through in the past few days, all she'd witnessed and learned, her concerns about Vaughn seemed less important than they had at the beginning of the week. That Vaughn still had feelings to resolve was obvious. Whether or not he chose to ask for Sydney's help in doing so might ultimately be better left to him. There were, in fact, only so many things it was good to feel you should be controlling. She didn't want to make demands of him. She wanted only to be there for him as the safe haven she felt he had always been for her. Pressing her body to his and feeling the warm, pleasant tingling as he wrapped his arms around her and gently kissed the top of her head, she'd found a semblance of peace. What mattered was that they had the time to be like this and that they would face side by side whatever might come. The rest would take care of itself . . . in time.

The address Sloane had given her belonged to a small stucco house on a suburban street situated directly across from a large tree-filled park. After circling the street to confirm the location, Sydney parked the rental car on the far side of the park, behind a thicket of trees. They got out of the car, clasped hands, and made their way slowly to a bench beneath the trees.

"So what are we doing here?" he finally asked.

"I just wanted to check on a friend," she replied evasively.

He took this in stride, seating himself beside her and placing an arm around her shoulder.

She fixed her gaze on the little yellow house, and he followed her eyes.

"It's nice," he said, then teased, "Thinking about retiring?"

"Nope," she replied. It was a warm day. In fact, in this part of the country most of the days would be warm, given it's proximity to the desert.

A nice touch, she allowed. This might be as close as anywhere in America could come to recreating the setting where Katelyn had spent her entire life. Sydney relaxed further when she caught site of an innocuous dark green sedan circling the street. To the casual observer this wouldn't have seemed unusual. To the trained eye this was one of many nonintrusive security measures that all of those in protective custody enjoyed.

Vaughn noticed the sedan too, and turned a questioning gaze on Sydney. A moment later his implied question was answered when the front door to the house opened and a tall, elegant woman with short silver hair emerged carrying a pair of gardening gloves and a small spade and trowel. She was followed by a shorter, plumper woman with long white hair pinned untidily to the top of her head. She wore a long flowered smock over her short-sleeved white T-shirt, and also looked ready for a day in the garden.

As they hemmed and hawed over landscaping alternatives, a shorter figure emerged from the side of the house, carrying a green bucket containing several trimmings of roses. Only once she had set the cuttings down could Sydney clearly make out Katelyn's smiling face. Her thick curls hung loosely, and she was dressed in well-worn jeans and a pink top.

Sydney smiled as Vaughn started to rise.

"Sydney, we have to get out of here," he said quietly.

"I know," she replied without moving.

"How did you find this place?" he asked.

"I just had to make sure," she said softly, still

unable to tear her eyes from the tranquility of the action she was witnessing, and wanting to allow her battered heart as much of the cooling balm that the sight was pouring into her.

"Do you have any idea who those women are?" she asked. She had read Dixon's report and had a good guess, but she knew that Vaughn could confirm their identity for her.

"I do," he replied. "And more important, they might know who I am."

"The neighbors?" Sydney asked.

Vaughn nodded.

"Would you sit down?" she finally said. "They can't see us back here, and even if they could, they wouldn't recognize us from this distance."

With a reluctant sigh, Vaughn complied, though Sydney noted that he kept his head down and angled toward her, just in case.

"I don't know," he said. "I can't vouch for Grace or Angel's eyes, but Katelyn is as sharp as anyone I've ever met. And the thing is she'd want to see you again. She really fell in love with you, after just a few hours together."

"Well, she's got great taste," Sydney teased. "And she's not the only one, right?"

Vaughn smiled that cocky half smile that Sydney loved so much, took her in his arms, and kissed her gently.

"You're something else, you know that?" he said.

"Sometimes," she replied.

"Pretty much all the time," he countered.

Sydney kissed him back, then, taking his hand, rose and led him back toward the car. She walked with a calm serenity that hadn't settled into place until she'd been able to confirm with her own eyes that Sloane had been as good as his word. Whatever the future held for Katelyn, she would be well protected, not just by the armed men and women who would regularly patrol the neighborhood, but also by the two women who had agreed to make Katelyn their world for the rest of their lives. And whatever the future held for Sydney, she could now face it secure in the knowledge that however much she had survived or had yet to endure, all in all, she had gained infinitely more than she had lost.

As he opened her door for her, Vaughn said, "Can I ask you something?"

"Sure," she replied.

"Eric and Nadia . . . ," he began hesitantly.

"What?" she asked, genuinely curious.

"It's just . . . do you think we're cold?"

"No." Sydney shook her head.

"Good," he said, kissing her on the cheek before he made his way to the passenger door.

"Why?" she demanded before he could get in.

"Just asking," he said, climbing in.

Sydney paused, then with an air of defiance reiterated, "We're not cold."

As she seated herself, Vaughn took her hand and brought it to his lips. Gazing hopefully into her eyes, he agreed, "I didn't think so."

ABOUT THE AUTHOR

Kirsten Beyer is a relative newcomer to the world of media tie-ins. *Star Trek Voyager, String Theory Book 2: Fusion* and the short story "Isabo's Shirt" from *Star Trek: Distant Shores* were her first forays into the world of professional publication. *Once Lost* is her first *Alias* novel.

In addition to her published works, Kirsten continues to work on her screenplays and original novels. She is also an actress with numerous plays and several TV and film appearances to her credit. She is a company member and performer with Unknown Theater and currently makes her home in Los Angeles with her husband, David, and their very fat cat, Owen.